THE *Dream Room*

WILLIAM MORROW *An Imprint of* HarperCollins*Publishers*

THE *Dream Room*

Marcel Möring

FIRST EDITION

Book design by Shubhani Sarkar

Photograph by Sean Kernan

Printed on acid-free paper

Library of Congress Cataloging-in-Publication Data has been applied for.

ISBN 0-06-621240-5

02 03 04 05 06 QW 10 9 8 7 6 5 4 3 2 1

For Sam

THE *Dream Room*

One

WHEN, IN A SUDDEN SURGE OF PRIDE, HE GAVE UP his old job without actually having a new one, my father decided to build model airplanes. The Doll Hospital, which was just downstairs, was constantly visited by boys who came for a plastic Messerschmidt kit or Spitfire Mark V, but as soon as they saw the ready-made models that were hanging from the ceiling most of them wanted one of those instead. I had been there when a couple of boys once asked if they could buy one of those finished models.

"They're not for sale," said the doll doctor. "They're here to show what it looks like. It's a kit. You're supposed to build them yourself."

He began talking louder when he spoke to these boys, like an English tourist in France who thinks that it's only a matter of speaking more slowly and loudly to make yourself understood.

"But I don't want to build them myself," the boys replied.

"What do you think?" roared the doll doctor. "You think I've got nothing better to do than spend the whole day building airplanes for you? Bugger off!"

He was a man of little patience.

Once a month, when he came up to collect the rent, the doll doctor would complain to my father. They'd sit in the old wicker chairs on the balcony that ran all along the back of the house, and drink beer. It was always evening when the doll doctor came.

"In my day we did everything ourselves. My father even made me my first bicycle, out of the parts from three old bikes. Nowadays those brats can't do a damn thing."

"Everything was better in the old days," said my father.

"God . . . How right you are." The doll doctor drank his beer and let out a deep moan.

"If you sold them ready-made," I said, "you could ask more money for them." I was leaning against the railing, looking out at the windows on the other side of the park behind our house. Sometimes, when my father and I were sitting on the balcony, we played a game: we tried to guess what they were doing and saying, in their little lamplit cubicles across the park. Usually it ended in some sort of radio play. "I told you not to dry your socks in the oven!" I'd shriek, and my father would slowly reply that drying socks in the oven was a better idea than making ice in a hot-water bottle (which I had tried once).

"I don't have time to build airplanes," said the doll doctor. "And I don't feel like it, either."

"I would let somebody else do it," I said, "and I'd give him a few guilders per box and add that to the price of the kit, plus a bit extra. Nobody sells ready-made model planes. I think the customer is perfectly happy to pay more for something like that."

"And who is supposed to build them for me?" asked the doll doctor. He sounded pensive.

I turned around. My father shook his head with a barely perceptible "no." The doll doctor followed my gaze.

"Boris! Damn! You're an aviator. If you . . . I'll give you a guilder a box."

My father sank back in his chair, groaning. I picked up my empty glass from the table and went inside.

"Why a guilder?" I heard my father say. "And what does my being a pilot have to do with it?"

"You can have fifty cents if you think a guilder is overpaid," said the doll doctor.

"If you want another beer . . . ?"

"Okay, one guilder fifty," said the doll doctor. "That's as high as I go. I have my margin to think of."

My father picked up the empty bottles and headed for the kitchen. "His margin," he said, as he passed me. I was sitting on a stool behind the bar, reading a cookbook. "He who will get rich because of him will never be poor again."

"I heard that!"

"You were supposed to," said my father. He ducked into the steaming mouth of the refrigerator. When he reappeared, he looked at me for a long time. I pushed my glass toward him. He straightened his back and walked past me. "I'm not talking to you, sir," he said. "You tricked me into this." The doll doctor laughed. I picked up my glass and went to the fridge. "That's the last one," said my father. "In my day, a boy of your age would have been in bed hours ago."

"Everything was better in the old days," drawled the doll doctor.

"Now he's telling me," said my father.

WHEN I CAME HOME from school the next day, the landing was packed with boxes with pictures of airplanes that rose up, grinning wickedly, out of grayish clouds of smoke, fire belching from their wings. The piles of cardboard were nearly up to my chin and formed a colorful wall of cardboard that ran from one end of the hallway to the other. On one of the piles stood a glass globe filled with water in which a tiny airplane was perched on a stand. There was a note from the doll doctor taped to the glass. My name was written on it. I took the globe in my hand. It began, hesitantly, to snow.

"For a man who sells children's toys, he really doesn't have a clue when to stop," said my father, when, half an hour later, he walked out onto the landing and found me there, amid the drifting piles of boxes. I still had my coat on and was sitting on the floor, the snow globe in my hand, dreaming about Hawker Hurricanes, Lancaster Bombers, and Focke Wulfs. "The boxes alone are good enough for you, aren't they?" He kneeled down beside me and drew a long, rectangular-shaped package from out of the pile. There was a DC-3 on it, in desert camouflage, flying improbably low over a dusty plain, where long lines of yellowish-brown jeeps left tracks in the sand.

"I used to fly a Dakota," said my father. "Just after the war, when they would let you fly anything that had wings." He stared over my head, at the shower curtain rods that were wedged between the side of the meter box and the living room wall and served as coatracks. I followed his gaze and saw him, young and tanned, cap askew, leaning out of the window of the plane as he was cracking a joke while the mechanic was inspecting the left propeller. A little farther down the sunlight bounced off the dull metal skin of the Nissen huts. High above the airstrip, where the tarmac disappeared into flat patches of dry grass, a small red spray plane turned its nose in the wind. "In those days, flying was just like riding a motorcycle," he said. "You jumped into your crate and took off, and if you got hungry you just set her down in a field behind a village pub to get a plate of fried eggs." He produced a thin smile and groaned as he got up. "Come on," he said. "Help me carry in a pile of these boxes. We're going to build a B-seventeen."

That night I made mushroom omelets, which we ate while gluing together the gray plastic pieces of airplane. The box had boasted a roaring flying fortress, her gun turrets spitting fire at viciously attacking Messerschmidts. What took shape in our hands, however, was a dull plastic lump with ugly welds. When the fuselage was finished, my father held it up doubtfully: "I'm beginning to understand why they all want to buy ready-made planes. This is a mess. What does he expect us to do next? Paint it?" In the hallway, next to the piles of boxes, I had seen a bag of tiny pots of paint and equally tiny brushes. When I told my father he grumbled to himself. "We'll be the Fords of the model airplane industry, then. If you file down the welds, I'll do the painting. We'll divide up the assembly per model."

I thought of the wall of cardboard out in the hallway. I wasn't really so sure that, after this B-17, I wanted to build more planes.

"Look, mate," said my father. "This was your idea and I'm perfectly willing to carry it out, but not on my own. If you want to get rid of that pile, you'll have to put your money where your mouth is."

I started to say something, but when I looked at him I saw he was dead serious. I stared down at the flotsam of plastic bits and pieces. If we went on at this rate we would have to assemble a plane every night for months to come. I looked at my father. My father looked at me. I sighed and lowered my head.

There was a stumbling noise on the stairs. The coat hangers clicked against the shower rods. My mother opened the door and stared at the mess on the table. "What's going on here? What are all those boxes doing in the hallway?" She looked disheveled. My father stood up and went over to her. He kissed her on the neck and turned around, so that they were both looking at me. "Be proud of your son," he said. "He has come up with a wonderful idea that's going to make us rich."

"How convenient," said my mother. "I just got fired." She wriggled out of my father's half-embrace, kissed me on the head, and looked at the airplane-in-the-making that stood between the empty plates. "What is that?"

"Fired?" There was a touch of concern in my father's voice.

"An airplane," I said. "We're building model airplanes for the doll doctor."

My mother looked from one to the other with an expression on her face as if we had just told her we were going to start a penguin farm in Greenland. "What did you have for tea?"

"Mushroom omelets," I said. "With fresh thyme."

"Did you let him cook again?" she said to my father.

"He's better at it than I am. Why were you fired?"

"Time for bed," said my mother. She laid her hand on the back of my neck and gave me a gentle squeeze. "They threw me out. For impertinence. I think I'm too old for this kind of work. I can't stand it anymore when an overgrown child with a little mustache who's just out of high school treats me like his slave."

"Oh, Lord," said my father.

I got up from my chair and let my mother lead me out of the room. As we passed my father he gave me a pensive look. He leaned down to kiss me good night. "That idea of yours," he said, "just became a plan."

MY PARENTS FIRST MET when my father was brought into the hospital with so many broken bones that the osteopath told the head nurse to phone a colleague who liked doing jigsaw puzzles. My mother, who had just received her degree and was standing for the first time as a full-fledged nurse at a patient's bedside, had failed to see the humor in it. She gazed at the tranquil face of the young man lying there on the white operating table and felt (highly unprofessional) compassion flooding her like a spring tide. His light, sun-bleached hair lay tousled on his forehead, and his face, despite the pain he must have felt before they had knocked him out, had the healthy complexion of someone who spent much of his time outdoors. No one in the hospital looked like that. No one she knew had his hair. And when they began to cut away his clothes she realized that she had never seen anyone with such a body. His limbs were bent where they shouldn't have been and the left side of his chest and pelvis showed the first signs of hemorrhaging, but all the same he looked so familiar that she immediately knew his name. She called him Boris. (Later, when he woke up and was able to speak again, his name turned out to be Philip. That didn't impress my mother. His parents had obviously made a mistake. This man was clearly a Boris. It was a name my father later accepted with pride, almost as if it was a mark of distinction, or a medal.)

My mother had become a nurse because of the war.

In 1944, just outside the village behind the dunes where she lived, a plane had crashed, and she and her friends had found the English pilot, still in his parachute, dangling from a poplar. He wasn't too far from the ground, so the girls could clearly see his eyes rolled back in pain. His injuries proved to be less serious than they had thought—nothing but a dislocated shoulder—but the experience had made a lasting impression on my mother. The helplessness she felt when she found the pilot made her decide to devote her life to caring for her fellow man, for the weak and the sick: she was going to be a nurse. Her father, the mayor of the village, pointed out that a smart girl like her could be a doctor if she wanted to, but that was something she firmly rejected. In my mother's eyes, doctors were unstable types who told young women to undress when all they had was a cold and roamed the dunes with the mayor, the local lawyer, and the vet, slurping noisily from pocket flasks and shooting helpless little rabbits. She was exaggerating, of course, but she wasn't off the mark. My grandfather was a hunting fanatic whose chief misfortune in life was that the queen had sent him to a village in the dunes, where there wasn't a decent deer to be found. And it was also true that he, as I was to discover on later visits, played bridge once every two weeks with the lawyer, the vet, and the village doctor, something that was really an excuse for heavy port and claret consumption. Whether the doctor actually did have his young patients undress for no medical reason, I don't know, but I had noticed, on the few occasions when we were in the village and met him at my grandfather's house, that he behaved rather nervously around my mother.

My mother was what you would call a formidable woman. Both feet planted firmly on the ground and as certain of where she came from as where she was going. Somehow she was able to convince those around her, at a time when many women still regarded themselves as loyal subjects to their husbands, that she was a free and independent person and quite capable of leading her own life.

But there was one thing she had forgotten to take into account; and that was her compassion, the way in which my father's hair fell across his forehead and the boyish innocence of his broken body. When the osteopath's scalpel made the first incision it was as if the knife penetrated her own skin, opened her flesh, laid bare her bones. Although this was not her first operation, she felt her knees shaking and before the first pieces of the jigsaw puzzle that my father's legs were could be put back together, my mother lay in the next room, on a sofa, recovering from the first and only fainting spell of her life.

My father had spent the war years in England. He was fifteen when the Netherlands were invaded and on the morning of May 10 he and his best friend found themselves on the grounds of the glider club, where men were taking down the wind socks and signposts in a naive attempt to prevent the enemy from landing. That was something that was, indeed, not to happen but most probably not because of the heroic resistance of the club members. The Germans seemed to have a lot more on their minds than capturing seventy yards of shorn grass and a couple of wooden sheds.

That morning my father, for the first time in his life, had had a fight with his father. They were standing in the sunny parlor listening to the radio, when my father said they should leave the country. My grandfather shook his head. He had a business to run, a firm that dealt in colorings and flavorings for the food industry, and he wasn't going to give up without a struggle everything he had built up over the last twenty years. He asked his son how he supposed they would survive in another country, with no money, no possessions, no chance of work or housing. "But that's exactly the point: survival," said my father. "Money and property are replaceable. Life is not." My grandfather had told him that he was being irresponsible, that *he* on the other hand had obligations toward other people, not just the family, but the people who worked for him. "They can save themselves!" my father had cried. My grandfather's eyes had blazed and he had said that he had always taken good care of his people and that now, now that things were really down to the crunch, he would keep on doing that. After that he had forbidden his son to speak anymore about the subject and my father stalked out of the door, angry and desperate, grabbed his bicycle, and rode to the glider field. On the way he saw people taping up the windows of their houses and packing suitcases into the trunks of their cars.

At the club they were busy dismantling the airstrips. The winch was still there at the end of the runway and his friend Benno, two years his senior, was standing beside it, waiting for the cart to take it away.

"I want to go up, just one more time," said my father suddenly.

"They'll never let you." Benno said.

"No, but I can do it if you help me. We might not be able to fly again for another three or four years."

"You'll be suspended if you fly without permission."

"What difference does it make, if I can't fly anymore anyway? Come on, Benno. Just once."

Benno looked around nervously. The governors were sitting in the wooden clubhouse drinking coffee and discussing the future. The sun was behind them and it was very unlikely that anyone would be able to see, with all that light in their eyes, what was going on farther down the airstrip. When they heard the winch starting up, they might come running. But by then it would be too late.

The boys ran to the hangar and rolled out the last plane that had been brought in. It was the chairman's plane, and it had been standing on the airstrip that morning, ready for takeoff, when the news came in about the invasion. As they lifted the slender wings and began pushing the plane out the door, Benno looked at my father over the top of the fuselage. "I know what you're doing," he said. My father, who didn't even know himself what he was doing, said nothing. "I'm going to be in trouble with the whole club and your whole family. This is Hendriks's plane, and he's the town clerk. What's he going to say when he sees you taking off . . ." The plane was now at the start of the airstrip. Benno ran to the winch to get the tow cable. My father lifted up the canopy and inspected the cockpit. When Benno came back and hooked him up to the cable, my father, who was beginning to understand what his friend had meant, said: "Why don't you come with me, Benno? Anything is better than staying." The other boy shook his head. "Somebody's got to work the winch. I don't want to run out on my family." They both stared down at the dry grass. Then Benno turned and started running back to the winch. My father crawled into the cockpit and shut the canopy.

Even before he felt the first tug of the cable, he began to have second thoughts. Leave his family . . . His father was right. He was responsible for the people who worked for him. The airplane slid across the grass and righted itself. He had to stay. He was responsible, too. He had to help his father. They can save themselves . . . How could he have . . . The plane cleared the ground. Benno, who was standing in the distance next to the winch, zoomed in closer. My father felt the explosion of pleasure in his stomach that he always felt when he was airborne. He was pressed back in his seat. He adjusted the trim, the airstrip disappeared under the nose of the plane, and he began climbing.

When he was free of the cable and looked back over his right wing he saw, far down below, over his shoulder, a tiny group of people standing between the clubhouse and the winch. Suddenly his doubts vanished. The field went shooting under him as he steered a course for the dunes, which were a distant yellow strip in the green countryside. Once he was flying over the sand he would use the updraft to gain height. It was a sunny day and there would undoubtedly be a thermal to give him the lift he needed for a good point of departure.

He reached England, though just barely. He had no map, navigated by means of the sun and his watch, but at the end of the day, flying dangerously low, the coast appeared and he managed, hungry, exhausted, dying of thirst, to set the glider down just outside a village. A month later he was taken in as a boarder by a Dutch family living in London and two years after that he began his training as a fighter pilot.

It was this training that enabled him to earn a living after the war: first flying a mail plane, later in the little planes that sprayed the endless fields of grain on the new land of the Zuider Zee Polders. Later still, when the country was prosperous again, he and his fellow pilots also flew over the smaller fields of farmers on old land where they'd dive down behind one row of trees, let the mist billow behind their wings, and then shoot back up, just before the next wooded bank. Those were the days when, as my father had told me, they'd land at noon in a meadow behind a village pub, climb out of the cockpit, and go inside for a plate of ham and fried eggs.

Different people will give different periods in their lives as a clear point in time, the moment when life itself suddenly seems simple and obvious, and when things and events seem to fit together with such ease that one will later wonder how on earth life could have been so obvious, what the secret was. There probably is no secret, it's the kind of memory, a memory that plays up more strongly than all the rest, a recollection tinged with melancholy and regret that makes one yearn for those days of freedom, the seeming wealth of possibilities, the first nudge in the back that later becomes the rhythm of life itself, grown-up life. For my father, that clear point in time was back in the days when he flew a spray plane. He never spoke about the war. He had fought in it, he had survived, he had known friendship and disappointment. For some strange reason those days, for him, were not colored by romantic notions. The few instances in which he spoke about his life as a fighter pilot, his mouth grew thin and tight and he invariably said that war was a filthy business. But in that spray plane, he felt better than ever before. He could do anything, he *did* everything, he saw everything, he knew everything. When he flew, his mind emptied and there was nothing but the thrust of the plane, the slow movement of his head to the left, glance over his shoulder, toward the swelling horizon, the green that filled his range of vision until he began to roll and the grass and the trees and the houses and the roads and the railroad tracks whirled around him in a haze.

One morning in June, after he had sprayed a potato field and was flying low over the roof of the adjacent farm, he saw the farmer's wife and her children standing on the gravel next to the barn. He picked up speed, rolled to the right (his least favorite side, but to the left was a row of tall poplars), and shot back across the field. Somewhere above the wooded bank that bounded the land, he brought up the nose until he felt the upward thrust fighting the downward pull. He kept on pulling the stick, looked left, and saw the horizon swerve. At the height of the loop, the engine sputtered. That often happened if the plane rose sheer for too long, the fuel pipes sometimes emptied. As soon as the nose was pointed down again, the kerosene would get to the engine.

But this time it didn't. The horizon tilted, the nose dropped, the engine remained silent. He pulled the stick back, aware that he had insufficient height to come back around if the engine didn't ignite. Then he heard it, the harsh roar. The nose went up; the potato field, which had been coming straight at him, went gliding under him. Now he was flying so low that the tops of the trees at the edge of the field seemed to tower above him. He threw the stick left and pulled it toward him. The wooded bank became a haze and disappeared. He had no time to look over his shoulder, but knew he was flying dangerously close to the ground. He pressed back in his seat, pulling hard on the control stick. Now he could no longer see the trees. He pulled a little more, moved the control stick to the middle and noticed that he only had a little speed left. The engine sputtered again and fell silent. He was now drifting crookedly over the field, at a height of ninety feet or so, a wooden fence before him, and behind him, a ditch, meadow, and cows. He pulled left slightly and kept on turning. The farm came into view again. Standing there, like tiny figures drawn in pencil, were the farmer's wife and her children. He could clearly see that they were waving. Five insect legs against the wall of the barn. He screamed with anger and helplessness, rammed his fist down on the start button, heard nothing, and yanked the stick to the right. The plane shot over the fence. Shortly afterward he felt the ground, the wild jolting as he bounced over the bumpy meadow. He could barely see in front of him and when the left wing hit a cow's head and he lost the last bit of control he had over the plane, he was so amazed that, for an entire second, he forgot everything else.

The rest of this unsuccessful crash landing passed him by. He heard the story later from the farmer's wife, who came with her husband to visit him in the hospital.

She hadn't realized that the pilot was no longer trying to entertain her and the children until the plane flew low over the fence and landed. Shortly afterward the cow went hurtling through the air, the plane spun around on its left wing, which was now dangling helplessly, seemed to make a pirouette, and crashed with its left side against the ground. When the farmer's wife got to the wreck, the right wing was sticking up proudly. The left half of the plane had carved a deep track through the grassy field. The pilot looked like a rag doll pressed against the back wall of the cockpit, his face caked with dirt.

In the weeks after the operation, my father looked like half a mummy. His left leg was in a cast up to his pelvis, as was his left arm. His chest was bandaged, the left side of his face was swollen and blue. The right side of his body was strangely unhurt. Anyone who happened to walk into his room saw what, to all intents and purposes, was a healthy man. But if they walked past the bed and looked back, they were surprised by the sight of a mummy swathed in plaster and bandages.

And so they met: the pilot who fell from the sky and the nurse who fell to the floor. Although she didn't actually work in the ward where my father lay, my mother could be found there whenever she was off duty. The head nurse, who caught her reading *Anna Karenina* to the patient during visiting hours, reported her curious behavior to the matron, but my mother said that the patient never had visitors, didn't seem to have any family, and that she didn't see the harm in keeping him company in her own free time. No one could think of anything to say against this. It wasn't until months later, when the two of them were found in the hospital garden, he in a wheelchair, she on the bench next to him, kissing with impassioned clumsiness, that it became clear to everyone that my mother was no Florence Nightingale and he, no Icarus. By that time, however, it was too late for moral indignation. He was soon to be discharged from the hospital, and that raised a completely new problem.

Before the accident, my father had rented two rooms from an old landlady in a village not far from the airstrip from which he and his mates took off to go spraying. There was no question of his going back there for at least the next six months. He walked on crutches, could barely take care of himself, and was in no shape to fly. A week before my father left the hospital, my mother, to the great surprise of the hospital staff, resigned, saying that she herself would care for him, in her parents' house in the dunes. And so the patient was driven to the village and helped up the stairs to the guest room. My father, who could offer no resistance against my mother's overwhelming decisiveness, spent the rest of his convalescence in that spacious, sunny room with the view of the dunes and the wide blue sky above the sea. He was not the first flier to recuperate there. The pilot whom my mother had seen hanging from his parachute in a tree years before had stayed in this same room and he had had the same nurse: the mayor's headstrong daughter.

Hardly a year after my father's spectacular admission to the hospital and my mother's equally spectacular response, they were to be found standing before the village mayor, who had the honor of joining his own daughter in holy matrimony.

The swelling under her wedding dress was, even to a practiced onlooker, imperceptible, but the bride's condition became apparent when, that night at the reception, she ran from the table (the appetizer was consommé julienne, something that would turn her stomach for the remaining seven months of her pregnancy) and, upon her return, began desperately eating pickles. By the time my mother finally looked up the party had completely fallen silent. She swallowed a last bit of pickle, dabbed at her mouth with the napkin, and smiled at her mother, her father, and, then somewhat uncertainly, at her new spouse. My father looked at her, leaned over, and kissed her on the mouth. Then he turned to the company and said, in such a gentle tone of voice that it was almost as if he were forgiving the guests for their awkward silence: "We shall call him David."

Until long after my birth, no one understood how my father could have been so sure that I would be a boy and how he had managed, that night, to silence the entire wedding party with such a simple remark. A sigh of relief went over the table. My grandfather, the mayor, stood up, raised his glass, and, glowing with pride and wine, drank a toast to his first grandson, while being tugged on the sleeve by his wife, who would never completely forgive her daughter for allowing herself to be impregnated under her own roof by a man who made his (undoubtedly meager) living flying spray planes.

A month before my birth, my father was well enough to fly again. But the thought of the child that was about to arrive and the memory of those waving insect legs against the barn, just as he was about to smash to bits against a cow, prevented him from taking up his old job again. Instead, he applied for a job as a salesman for a compressor manufacturer, while studying mechanical engineering in the evening. Eventually he became a kind of inventor who would work for a while for one firm, devise a machine that would render him superfluous, and then go looking for the next firm where he could bring about his own dismissal. My mother had given up her job as a nurse after my birth, but started working again when the peculiarities of my father's career became apparent. And now she, too, had proved incapable of holding a job. My idea, assembling model airplanes to supplement the family income, had indeed become a plan. It was the plan that would save us.

Two

AND SO WE STARTED BUILDING MODEL AIRPLANES. Despite the fine weather—it was a warm spring and the evenings were long and balmy—we sat from early morning till late at night working away on Hawker Hurricanes, Spitfires, Mosquitoes, B-17s, and Lancaster Bombers. All over the house were model planes in various stages of completion. My father had strung a wire from one end of the room to the other, from which we hung the models when they were finished. The bar was covered with freshly painted planes and the table strewn with fuselages and wings, wheels and elevators. When I came home from school my parents had already done half a day's worth. Usually we'd have a cup of tea on the balcony and I'd tell them about what had happened at school that day, and then we'd sit down at the table and get to work. We each had our own place in the assembly line. I unpacked the boxes, took out the larger pieces, and glued them together while my mother assembled the smaller parts and my father filed and painted the finished planes and added the insignia. We lived in a bubble where everything was quiet and sheltered and friendly; the pot of tea steamed over on its little candle, the sounds from the park behind our house drifted in through the wide open balcony doors. Once I bent down to pick up a wheel and saw that my mother had crossed her leg over my father's. His hand lay high up on her thigh. Her shoe lay on the floor and she was stroking his calf with her stockinged foot.

I remember that time with the same keen vividness as my father recalled his days as a spray plane pilot.

A week or two after we had started building, the weather turned and the rains began that were to last all summer long. Most mornings when we woke up, we heard the rain pelting down on the windowpanes and often it wouldn't let up until late in the afternoon. It never really got cold, but I still wore a jacket to school, hood up, Wellington boots on my feet. In the corridors, outside the classrooms, it stank of wet clothes and damp shoes and usually we stayed inside at break times, hanging around in the corridors or eating our sandwiches at the grubby Formica tables in the cafeteria. The older students congregated in the bathrooms and smoked secretly in the stalls, which meant we had to hold it in until they'd had their last cigarettes and gone back to their classrooms. One boy in my class complained, but after he had had his arm twisted behind his back and his head held under the tap, we waited patiently in line until the seniors left.

In the afternoons I'd walk back home through the tail end of a shower, trying to avoid the ankle-deep puddles that had been lying there for days and seemed as if they would never go away. It rained so hard and so long that the water in the canals rose above the stone embankment and soaked the grass. In some places, the stones had been washed away and it looked as if some gigantic water beast had taken bites out of the quayside. The trees were black with water, the streets were flooded, and one time it hailed so heavily that people on the street, their faces contorted in pain, ran for shelter in doorways and shops.

They were rains from distant lands. Sometimes I'd be walking home after school and the air would be filled with scents from across the sea, from other continents. One day it would smell of orange peel, another day, of asphalt, pebbles, cedar, sea, mountains, sheep, or barefooted young girls. Sometimes there was a thunderstorm and I'd wait, with several other pedestrians, in a doorway until it had stopped thundering and lightning. After that the city always smelled like freshly washed linen.

Our house wasn't holding up too well. The doll doctor had already come around three times to check the roof and one night in the middle of a downpour he and my father crawled through the attic window to clear dead leaves out of the drainpipe and check the lead. Pale brown snails' trails ran down the wall of my bedroom and in the stairwell was a stain that looked like a map of Russia.

My father suffered as much from the incessant showers as our house did. Now and then, when we were building planes, the room so dark that we had to turn on all the lights, he would stand up and go to the window. As my mother and I glued and filed, he'd look outside, hands in his pockets, shaking his head, his shoulders hunched as if, even here inside, he could feel the damp and the chill. He was strangely silent. Sometimes he'd stare, without even seeing it, at a half-painted plane on the table before him, and for minutes at a time he'd do nothing.

One afternoon I came home from school and when I got to the top of the stairs I saw, through the window that separated the hallway from the kitchen, my parents, at the breakfast bar: my father was standing in the kitchen, my mother sat on the other side of the bar, on a stool. My mother was talking, my father wasn't looking at her. He was leaning over the bar, shuffling through a stack of paper. ". . . model airplanes," I heard my mother say.

"Boris, look at me! You can't go on avoiding everything. This isn't making you happy, either." He looked up and grinned. "Happiness," he said, as if he had just heard a good joke for the first time in years.

I opened the door and went inside. Neither of them appeared to see me. It was completely silent. Then, after what seemed like a long, long time, my father turned his head toward me. He swept together the sheets of paper and said: "Back to work." My mother's eyes rested on him briefly, as if she were waiting for an answer, and then she got up from her stool.

That evening, but it was probably nighttime by then, I woke up to the sound of their voices. They weren't speaking particularly loudly, they weren't having a fight, nor was there anything in the tone of their voices that disturbed me, but all the same, I woke up. Although I couldn't understand every word they said, I knew that the conversation was a continuation of the one I had interrupted that afternoon. I listened for a while to the murmur of their voices and then fell back to sleep.

The next morning, when I was standing in the bathroom brushing my teeth, my mother walked in. She turned on the shower and held her hand out to check the temperature. I rinsed my mouth, dried myself off, and asked what we would do when there were no more boxes. Behind her, steam was billowing up out of the shower stall. She stepped into the mist, tipped back her head, and closed her eyes.

"Is he going to fly again?"

She straightened her head. Her face was patterned with glistening rivulets. She brushed the water out of her eyes and gave me a penetrating look. "Fly?" she said. "No, I don't think so. Why do you ask?"

I turned to the mirror and looked at the patches of steam that made everything seem hazy and far away.

"Everything comes to an end," said my mother.

I drew my fingers through the film on the glass.

My mother, her voice barely audible over the splattering of the water, began humming.

That night I heard their voices again, but I was so sleepy I couldn't understand what they were saying.

THE NEXT DAY I came home from school, and my father was sitting alone at the table. The familiar display of finished and half-finished planes was gone. He sat up straight, in his usual chair, smiling absently into space. For a long time he didn't even seem to notice me. It wasn't until I had made tea and poured us each a cup that he snapped out of his trance. He held his head to one side and grinned a John Wayne–like grimace.

"What are these?" he said, pointing to the dish I had set down in front of him.

"Scones," I said. "I baked them yesterday, but they're still fine, I think."

"Scones . . ." he said. "What's going to become of you?"

"Where's . . ."

"Job-hunting."

"Job . . ."

What had been the start of a grin now crinkled into a full-fledged smile. "She's going to fly."

I stared at him. My mouth fell open.

My father began laughing, as if he suddenly saw the humor in it. "She's applied for a job as a stewardess." He laughed harder and harder. I looked at him. I couldn't help it, I started laughing too.

"She's going to fly!" My father slammed his hand down on the table. The teapot jumped and the candle flickered in the tea warmer. He howled with laughter. I howled with laughter. We lay facedown on the table, our heads buried in our arms, and laughed until we cried.

And then, all at once, there was silence. I sat up, my cheeks damp from laughing, and as I stared at my father, who was still grinning and wiping his eyes, I suddenly remembered what my mother had said, that everything must come to an end, and there, at that moment, the feeling I had had for the past few weeks suddenly vanished, that sense that we were living in a bubble, that we had landed in a place in time where we were safe and sheltered, invulnerable to sorrow and woe . . . I looked at my father. The last trace of a grin faded from his lips, the sparkle in his eyes faded.

MY FATHER AND I finished off the last few planes together. We sat at the table and silently passed each other parts. Now and then, whenever a new box was opened, my father would tell me something about the model, that the Messerschmidt 110 was a slow turner, for instance, but was dangerous to attack because of the tail gunner, and then we'd look at the picture on the box before we went on, sorting parts, filing wings, gluing, and painting. I gazed at the shrinking pile in the hallway like a prisoner who was counting the days that separated him from freedom.

And then, one day, I came home from school and the pile was gone. As I peeled off my wet clothes next to the coat rack I heard a metallic rattling coming from the living room. I stood among my dripping things and listened intently. A bell tinkled. I lowered my jacket and schoolbag to the floor and walked carefully toward the living room door.

My father was sitting at the breakfast bar. Before him, in a sea of crumpled paper, stood the old portable typewriter. A cigarette lay in an ashtray. Smoke curled up lazily to the ceiling. My father greeted me wearily and pointed to the teapot, standing over a flame. He stuck the cigarette in the corner of his mouth and continued typing. The bell tinkled and he pulled back the carriage, blew out smoke, and hammered away at the keys. After a while, he stopped. I sat across from him, on the other side of the typewriter. He had stubbed out his cigarette and drank large gulps of tea. It was a long time before either of us spoke.

"We can't go on making planes forever, boy." He looked at the sheet of paper hanging out of the typewriter. "Though I must say, I think I'm better at building planes. When you have to describe your life in a few lines, it all seems like nothing more than chance and coincidence."

"What do you do for a living?"

My father looked up with an expression that bordered on amazement. "God," he said after a while. Faint lines rippled across his forehead. There was a long silence.

"I'm going to go do my homework," I said.

"Wait! Wait." He frowned, then shook his head. "I . . ."

Suddenly I saw him again as the flier, the model airplane builder, the engineer who invented machines that made him unnecessary. I was standing next to my stool, half turned away. Faces, each one slightly different than the last, slid in front of the other. One man, so many faces.

"What do *you* want to be, when you grow up?" he asked.

"A cook," I said.

"I thought as much. Do you really want to be a cook? Is that the only thing you really want?"

"I do now," I said. "But perhaps it's not what I imagined."

"Nothing is," he said. "It never is."

We looked at each other for a while.

"Nothing ever is all that great." He raised his hand, as if to stop any objections. "But that's not the point. You have to hold on. If you really want something, you have to hold on to it. That's at least as important as talent."

"But . . ."

He took out a cigarette and lit it. In the cloud of smoke that poured from his mouth, he said. "Did I ever tell you what I did after the war?"

He had come back and started flying for spray companies. And then he had had that accident.

"No, before I came back. I stayed in England for a while." He beckoned. "Sit down a minute."

I poured fresh tea and he told me how, in those days, victory had come, an end to the war, and how he had discovered that his life, from one moment to the next, was no longer a path paved by circumstances outside himself. "It was," he said, "as if there was an empty plain in front of me, and I knew that I had to go out into that emptiness. At least, that's what I supposed life was: an expedition to the South Pole, but *before* Amundsen and Shackleton had set foot there, New Zealand before Tasman, South Africa before Van Riebeeck."

Like so many exiles, he reported weekly to the Dutch embassy, in the hope of getting news of his parents. Most of the others were *Engelandvaarders*, men who were often somewhat older and who, during the war, had crossed the North Sea in anything that could float, determined, hell-bent on driving out the enemy. Whenever he sat among them on a bench, waiting his turn, he felt as if he were the complete opposite of them.

In the months that followed, the row on the bench in the stately white embassy building grew smaller and smaller. Finally, he and a chain-smoking playboy in blue blazer and silk scarf were the only ones left. They sat across from each other, in silence.

One day the other man opened his mouth and said,

nodding at the book in my father's hand: "Writer?" My father shook his head: "Reader." The man laughed. "A strange bunch, we exiles. Writers, adventurers, war-horses, and weaklings, but not a normal person among us." My father knitted his brows and tried to think whether he knew a writer living in London. "I, person-ally, am one of the weaklings," said the playboy. He stood up and held out his hand: "Paul van Zevenbergen ter Borgh." My father got to his feet and returned the handshake. The man nodded when he heard his name. "So, not a writer, but not an adventurer either. Not a warhorse, I assume. You are like me: you fled because you had something to fear." He paused, then continued. "I myself fled because the new ideology had a bit of trouble with the notion that one could love a member of his own sex." It was a while before my father under-stood what the man meant. "The fundamentals of Gre-cian culture," Van Zevenbergen explained. "That's what my father used to call it. I'm hoping they can tell me what has happened to my dear friend Charles van Dongen. He was an actor. I am . . . was . . . an antique dealer. I happened to be here on business when all the trouble began. Cigarette?"

They smoked.

"I didn't actually flee," said my father. He told him of how he had left. Van Zevenbergen listened, smiling. When my father was finished, he crossed his arms and looked at the young man before him. "Dear fellow," he said. "You may not have fled intentionally, but you knew, just as I did, that you were better off getting out of there. Listen. It makes no sense to sit here waiting. If your parents, like so many others, have been transported east, it may be quite some time before they show up on the lists. As far as the Dutch government is concerned, they're displaced persons. Sometimes they aren't even treated as Dutchmen. I've heard stories . . . Go to the Netherlands and look for them. Here . . ." Van Zevenbergen drew a small card out of his pocket, found a pen, and scribbled something. "Take this. There's a booking office, I'll jot down the name and address, a friend of mine works there. He'll help you."

"But what about you? Why don't you go back?"

Van Zevenbergen smiled. "Let's just say I'm a bit of a fatalist. But if you ever hear anything about an actor named Charles van Dongen, I hope you'll . . ."

My father nodded and shook his hand.

But Van Zevenbergen wasn't the only one who was a bit of a fatalist. My father just couldn't bring himself to make the crossing and return home. He feared both his parents' reproaches and their possible fate, and he convinced himself that he wasn't avoiding the one but awaiting the other and that, as long as his letters were left unanswered, he'd be better off in London.

Through someone at the embassy who was in charge

of trade he came in contact with Dutch companies that were trying to restore their business relations in Great Britain, and from then on he continued to visit the embassy for his work, meanwhile casting his weekly glance on the lists of missing persons and victims. Van Zevenbergen, however, never showed up again.

One morning he presented himself at a seedy little office in the Edgware Road. He was shown in by the secretary, a woman in her late fifties, who gave him a mug of tea and cleared off a few piles of paper from a little wooden bench so he could sit down. She herself sat down, with a weary smile, at her overcrowded desk and began pecking nearsightedly at the keys of her typewriter. The walls were covered with yellowed posters showing what must have been every cogwheel and bearing that Morris & Sons had manufactured since the start of the Industrial Revolution. Among the posters were a map of the Middle East and another of the Continent. Here and there, little red flags had been stuck into the map of Europe. Many people had kept track of the Allied armies' progression on maps such as these. My father stood up, teacup in hand, to get a better look. There were a surprising number of flags and they were stuck in awkward places. The British and American armies had never advanced that far. The secretary had stopped typing. He looked at her, about to ask something, when the door of the office swung open. There stood a heavyset man with bushy eyebrows and the wild remains of what must once have been a striking head of hair but was now a corona of gray flames around a gleaming bald pate. He leaned his left hand against the doorjamb and looked at my father with a gaze so intense that he shrank back slightly. The secretary bent over her typewriter again to search for a new letter. With a nod of his head the man beckoned, and they entered the office.

The mass of paper on the rolltop desk against the wall was so huge, and, judging from its discoloration, so old, that it seemed highly unlikely, or at least not for a good ten years yet, that Morris & Sons would ever be eligible for the title "Most Efficient Company in England." The man with the wide wreath of hair sat down at an empty wooden table, spread two plump hands on the tabletop, leaned back, and regarded the visitor from under his heavy eyebrows.

"Godawful mess in here," he said, without averting his gaze.

"Well . . . I don't . . ."

"An internal mess." The man turned halfway around, toward the cluttered rolltop. "On the left are notes and letters from over a hundred correspondents. All still need to be typed out." He turned back to his visitor. "Mrs. Singer is not, as you may have noticed, the fastest typist in the world." He moved to the other side. "This pile here, this is the finished material and over there . . ." He was facing his visitor again. ". . . there, behind you, against the wall, in those files, are the company records. All our cogwheels and bearings and God knows what rubbish. I'll be honest with you, Mr. . . ."

My father told him his name.

The man was silent for a moment. "I'll be honest with you. This company is a joke. We exist . . . We *survive*, I should say, thanks to the generosity of a few old buyers, customers who were always treated well by my father and his brother and who'd be ashamed to turn their backs on us now."

My father, who was still holding his mug, began to feel uncomfortable, and took a sip of his cold tea.

"My mind is not on it anymore. Nearly everything we earn, and that isn't much, goes into the investigation."

"Investigation?"

The man got up from his chair, leaned heavily on the table, his face stony, and said: "The map you were looking at. What do you think it was about?"

My father tried to look the man in the eye, but had

to turn away. "The Allies," he said. "The Allies' progress." He thought for a moment. "But the flags are in the wrong places."

The man jerked upright and pulled open the bottom drawer of a filing cabinet. He took out a bottle and two smudged glasses. Without asking his guest if he drank—and at this hour of the day no less—he poured three fingers of whiskey in each. He set one glass down on the table and took a swig of the other. "The Germans' progress, rather," he said. "Each flag stands for a camp, a concentration camp. Interesting name, when you think about it." He sat back down and swirled the whiskey around in his glass. "What did they concentrate there? Perhaps we should interpret the concept of 'concentration' the way it's used in chemistry: a process by which a substance is stripped of all its diluents and extraneous material, until only the essence . . . no, the soul . . . until only the soul of that substance remains." He drank. He drank calmly and controlledly. Not the drinking of a drinker, my father thought. "So. Every flag is a camp, where European Jewry was concentrated down until nothing remained but its soul."

"I . . ."

"Yes, I know what it is you want to say. You have no business here. Your Dutch clients are looking for professional, reliable companies that can deliver on

time and according to specifications. And you're abso-
lutely right: you have no business here. My sons had no
business in Germany, either. I tried to talk them out of
it. But my wife's family was still living there, somewhere in Frankfurt, and they were going to get them
out. Who would hurt an Englishman? We weren't even
at war yet."

"I'm sorry . . ."

"Drink your whiskey, Mr. Speijer. It's not every
day that I open this bottle, and as far as I know it's a
good one."

My father drank his whiskey, without finding out if
it really was, as Mr. Morris said, a good one.

"They arrived at the house of my wife's brother
when the . . . riffraff . . . was throwing the furniture out
the windows and carrying off the valuables in pillow-
cases. And before they knew it, they got carried off
themselves. They were rowers, my boys, Adam and
David, though they weren't allowed on the university
team. Muscular young men. They were up against a
kind of hostility they'd never known. And what do they
do? They roll up their sleeves to . . . to drive out that
scum. But these weren't just a band of hooligans, sir.
They were the official representatives of the German
government and they did what they'd been told: purge a
Jewish home. My sons were arrested, beaten, and Lord

knows what else and taken off to a camp where they were concentrated, until all that was left was their soul. And that is what keeps this company busy. We'll sell a box of cogwheels—for a song and dance, if we have to—and pay our correspondents to find out everything they can about concentration, how it all worked, the technical side, the where and when and how. Not the why— no. That's the easiest answer of all. And now, if you've finished your whiskey, you may leave."

But my father did not leave. He stayed and listened to Mr. Morris. He stayed until the sun sank and orange light shone through the dusty windowpanes and the blood pounded in his temples. He stayed until it gradually dawned on him that he didn't know what kind of a war he had fought in until he knew of the terrible world in which he had left his family behind seven years before. He stayed until all he could do was leave. The next day when he visited the embassy to make arrangements for his journey home, the names of his parents had appeared on the Red Cross list.

We sat side by side at the bar, where the typewriter stood and the ashtray with the cigarette butts.

"And then I came back. You know the rest." He poured tea and handed me my mug. We drank in silence. I felt an endless weariness settling down on me.

"So if you ask me what I do for a living, I'd say I'm

still looking for something as powerful as Mr. Morris's need to find out everything he could about concentration."

I nodded.

"Something real," he said. "One has to do something real."

I didn't know if cooking fell into that category. I began thinking about that.

"On your feet," said my father. "You've homework to do."

I was standing by the door when he called out to me again. I turned around. He sat there behind the bar, his hands on the keys of the typewriter, looking like the kind of writer you saw in Hollywood movies. "Career," he said. "How do you spell career?"

I DIDN'T KNOW IF I would ever become a cook, and I didn't have the faintest idea if it was real, or even important, but one thing was certain: nearly all my thoughts revolved around cooking and eating. My mother, who observed my fussing about in the kitchen with a mixture of admiration and concern, claimed that it was all Humbert Coe's fault, and although he had undoubtedly had something to do with my culinary fervor, I knew there was another reason.

There are people who think in three dimensions, who immediately see objects in relation to their surroundings: they might become architects. Other people are good at breaking down objects and images, visually, into their various components. Alberto Giacometti once described such an experience. He had been desperately searching for the right way to paint eyes, and one afternoon, tired of thinking, he went to see a Laurel and Hardy movie. At a certain point he realized, to his amazement, that the image on the screen had broken down into black and white segments and that he was no longer seeing figures and backgrounds, but compositions of light and dark planes. After that he was able to paint his famous portraits.

Something similar happened to me, with food. One day we were eating a sauerkraut casserole that tasted different than usual. I asked my mother what she had done, but she was unaware of having done anything special. As she was telling me this, the taste broke down, in my mind, into its components and I knew she had used cumin. When I asked her this, she frowned, then remembered that she had, in fact, on the advice of the greengrocer, added cumin to the sauerkraut.

But it was true that Humbert Coe had had something to do with it.

In a certain sense his influence began before I was

born. That was a long time ago, during the war, when he taught my father to eat Marmite, had him taste wines that most people would never be able to taste again and explained to him how one could recognize a good restaurant and what day of the week one should eat there. Because of this I was the only child who took Marmite sandwiches to school, was given, at an early age, a glass of wine on festive occasions, and would, for the rest of my life, find it hard to dine out on a Monday.

The first time Humbert Coe came to the house, I didn't actually meet him. I only *heard* him.

One night I was woken up by the doorbell. My father stumbled down the stairs to the front door. There was a long silence, then a cry, unintelligible but clearly surprised. Two pairs of feet came up the stairs, the living room door opened, and I heard my father's voice. He was laughing. I hadn't heard him sound so cheerful in ages.

I lay there for a while wondering who it was and why my father sounded so happy, but soon sleep drew me back into her warm, dark embrace and everything faded away.

The next morning there was a man sitting at breakfast who was so enormous that I stopped dead in the doorway. The doors to the balcony were open and a gentle breeze blew in, smelling of freshly mown grass and morning dew. The stranger smiled the indulgent smile of a fat man. He leaned back slightly in his chair, placed his hands on the tabletop, and spread his fingers. They were big hands, and his fingers were plump, yet at the same time they were the hands of a man who knew how to touch things—and people—with tenderness. He wore a light-colored suit and a sumptuous, high-necked burgundy waistcoat that on anyone else would have looked pretentious but, on him, only emphasized what he was: a man who demanded quality, without reservation.

"You," he said, as one of the fleshy fingers moved and seemed to be pointing at me, "you must be young . . ."

"Have you two met?" My father was standing in the doorway. He gave me a nudge in the back. I went up to shake the visitor's hand. "This is Humbert Coe. We've known each other since the war."

I couldn't imagine this big man sitting in the cramped cockpit of a Hurricane or a Spitfire. Even if they had given him a Mosquito . . .

"I was a bit more slender in those days," said the visitor, who saw my frown.

My father laughed. "Mr. Coe wasn't an airman. He was a spy."

Coe roared with laughter. "Spy . . . You mean,

someone who was unfit to do anything useful and was dropped behind enemy lines in the hope that he would find something there to keep him occupied. The very word 'espionage' reminds me of Manhattans, hard-boiled eggs with Beluga . . ."

"Humbert, everything reminds you of Manhattans and hard-boiled eggs with Beluga."

They laughed.

Coe flipped open a cigarette case and held it out to my father. As they were lighting up, he tapped his cigarette lightly against the case. I stared at him, but he didn't seem to mind. There was a contented smile on his lips. He looked like the kind of man who was accustomed to having people stare at him, and who had not only grown used to it, but even come to appreciate it.

The smell of fried eggs drifted in from the kitchen. My mother had already set plates out on the table and poured coffee. Behind her, the frying pan sputtered and crackled on the stove.

My father and Coe talked. The visitor held his head to one side as he listened. Everything he did, breathing out smoke from his cigarette, listening, smiling, watching, drinking, he did with care. He was slow, but his slowness seemed to be the sort of deliberation that stemmed from an inherent need, or one developed over the course of many years, for the sake of precision.

The plates on the table were filled, fresh coffee was poured, the cigarettes were stubbed out. We were just about to begin eating when the visitor folded his hands, bowed his head, and sank into a brief silence. I regarded him with amazement. When Coe looked up, he sought my eyes and winked. My father, who had seen the wink, grinned and said: "I'll bet you two have a lot to talk about, Humbert. This boy is on his way to becoming the family cook."

The fat man arched one eyebrow.

"Julia still isn't too keen on the idea."

My mother pursed her lips.

"She thinks a boy his age should go to school and learn things, not stand around in the kitchen cooking."

Coe nodded thoughtfully. "Twelve? Thirteen?"

"Twelve," I said.

He let his head rock back and forth in approval. "That's the age when it happens. When did you begin to fly, Philip?"

My father mumbled something about "expensive hobby," but admitted that from the time he was eleven you could nearly always find him sitting on the fence around the glider field. Coe leaned back contentedly.

"A talent," he said, "is, at the start, nothing more than a somewhat obsessive interest. But with careful guidance, it can develop into that exceptional skill to which we generally refer when we speak of talent."

My father stared at him for a while. Then he turned to me. "When Humbert was still on our base, he would hang around the kitchen all day pestering the cooks. He used to say that the misery of war was no justification for half-cooked potatoes."

They laughed.

"But it's true, Philip," said Coe. "Certainly in times of need, food prepared with care can be a great consolation. It is my fate that I had to be raised in England, where the art of cooking is rarely taken seriously. Even though the British gastronomic culture has brought forth such magnificent dishes! Need I elaborate on Yorkshire pudding? The summer puddings with fresh fruit and bread fingers that dear old Cook used to make each summer? Warm scones with clotted cream? Potted salmon!"

"Humbert . . ."

He lifted his eyes and slowly returned from his dream of past delights. It was several moments before I realized that everyone at the table was looking at me. I was staring at the visitor, and my mouth was slightly opened. Coe studied me for a while and then began nodding, slowly at first, and then with the determination of someone who has thought up a good solution to a problem that has yet to be acknowledged as one. "Young man," he said. "You and I are going out for dinner this evening." He turned to my mother and lightly inclined his great head. "That is, if you will permit me, just this once, to take this young cook under my wing." My father grinned. My mother frowned. "He's still at school . . . This is an important year, the first year . . ."

Coe whipped the yolk out of his egg and maneuvered it onto a piece of bread. "School comes first," he said. "But if I'm not mistaken, it's nearly summer vacation. And *one* evening . . ."

"Let them go, Julia. It'll be a good experience for the boy. What do you think?" He looked at me. I nodded, gravely enthusiastic. My mother produced a faint smile.

"All right," she said. "All right."

"LEJEUNE," SAID COE that evening, as we crossed the canal in front of our house and walked into town, "is actually called De Jong. That is important information. It tells us that Mr. De Jong apparently doesn't have enough confidence in the quality of his business to work under his own, inconsequential name."

He was wearing a hat with a pearl-gray band and flourishing an ebony walking stick with a silver handle. I hoped we wouldn't meet anyone I knew.

"Lejeune is, at present, the best restaurant in town,

but Mr. De Jong seems to have his personality working against him. He insists that his customers order in French. Otherwise, he claims, you might as well stay at home and have fish and chips for dinner. And he'll walk straight up to a table to explain to a guest, in a voice loud enough for everyone to hear, the proper way to eat asparagus. Anyone who dares to order the wrong wine is taught a lesson right there at the table. Mr. De Jong, I think we can safely say, is a bit of a parvenu."

"How *are* you supposed to eat asparagus?"

"With your hands," said Coe. "Preferably from a napkin, while supporting the asparagus spear with a fork. Dreadful mess, and practically no one who can do it well anymore. As far as I'm concerned, you simply eat them with a knife and fork. Although . . . I did once see a young woman eating asparagus . . ." He placed the tips of his index and middle fingers against his thumb and gently kissed them. "I was referring to the young lady," he said, flicking me a glance. "She wore a Cossack hat, which, fortunately, she kept on at the table, and she was the only one of her party who consumed her asparagus in the proper fashion." He looked sideways and raised his eyebrows. "Are you shocked?"

"No."

"Good. A man who is easily shocked cannot taste." He gazed into the distance for a moment, his head tipped back slightly, as he strolled along, swinging his walking stick. "She wore a short black dress with nothing underneath. Mind you: one didn't see that, one knew it."

Now I was shocked. I wasn't sure I really liked seeing a man Coe's age so obviously relishing, as he himself probably would've described it, the beauty of a young woman.

"And she was hired."

I stopped short. Coe walked a few steps farther and then turned around. "Come, young man. We mustn't be late. Yes yes, come. Hired. It does happen. There are prostitutes, and there are ladies whose company one can enjoy at a reasonable fee. She belonged to the latter category."

"Where was that?" I asked warily.

Coe laughed. "Not here. Not at Lejeune. Don't worry. It was in London."

"How come you can speak Dutch?"

We turned right and crossed a square that lay, gleaming like a tortoiseshell, under the light of the streetlamps. Outside the entrance to a town house, two men were having a silent conversation. One of them was making short, stabbing gestures in the air with a lit cigarette.

"I am the result of a marriage between a Dutch

mother and a British father. Here, in this city, is where I grew up. That is to say, I lived here until the age of six or seven. Then we returned to England. My mother . . ." His voice acquired a tenderness that surprised me. "My mother loved to speak Dutch with me. She was a lonely woman. Just like your mother."

I opened my mouth, but no sound came out.

"My father sent me to boarding school. From then on it was the usual route. Cambridge, in my case. The classics, that was to be my . . . ah . . . future. *Et in Arcadia Ego*. Yes. *Brideshead Revisited*, that sort of thing." He made a gesture with his left hand as if he were shooing away an insect, only in slow motion. "Dutch Englishmen, English Dutchmen, they are an exceptional breed. Ever read Ford Madox Ford's *Parade's End*? No, probably not. You're a bit too young. Learn English, young man. I'll give you the book as a present. Tietjens, the protagonist, is just such an Englishman, of Dutch descent. Like Tadema, the painter."

I was trying desperately to remember everything, the names he mentioned, the book titles, the right way to eat asparagus, and that elegant young lady in a Cossack hat . . . it was a whirlwind of words, names, and thoughts.

"Ah, here we are. Now listen carefully."

We were standing in front of a richly ornamented

mansion whose windows glowed with festive yellow light. There were people sitting at tables, waiters walking back and forth carrying trays. In the marble foyer stood a boy who couldn't have been much older than I was. He wore a suit like an organ grinder's monkey and was thumbing mindlessly through a small pile of paper on a mahogany table.

"I haven't come here simply to treat you to dinner. I expect you to learn something. And another thing . . ." He paused, as if to convince me of the importance of his mission. "It is my job to eat in this sort of restaurant and then write about it. That is why we mustn't let anyone know that we are not like the other guests. From this moment on, you are my young nephew. I am your uncle."

I grinned so broadly that, for a brief moment, Coe looked at me in amazement. Then he nodded. "Come," he said, "gird yourself for battle, Telemachus."

After Coe had refused a small square table against the wall, saying we hadn't come here to play cards, we were seated at a spacious, round table in the middle of the room. Although he had emphasized the confidential nature of our mission, this apparently didn't mean we had to be inconspicuous. Not that there was much chance of that. Coe's entrance made many heads turn. Coe's detachment was contagious.

My mother had squeezed me into a jacket that had once been my father's and looked strangely aristocratic, an impression that was enhanced by the bow tie she had knotted around my neck before we left the house. But any discomfort I might have felt disappeared the moment I entered the dining room. Coe's presence, the combination of self-confidence and imperturbability he exuded, was so irresistible that I thought of all the reasons I could have for not caring what the rest of the world thought of me.

I was just a boy, at the end of my first year of secondary school, raised somewhat carefully by a father who wasn't very interested in the world and a slightly absent mother, but there were some things I did know. My father had taught me to read and speak English at a very early age (probably because he himself could barely speak the language when he flew over in his glider) and my mother had raised me with the notion that everyone had to fend for himself. The result was that now, on the eve of my thirteenth birthday, I could cook, do the laundry, mend clothes, and speak English. What she hadn't counted on was that I would come to love cooking, so much so that, for the past two or three birthdays, my parents had felt obliged to give me cookbooks. (And I read them. I read them the way other people read novels, and if I read a novel I preferred the ones in which there was eating and drinking, so I could convert the dishes and meals into recipes. My mother had once told me that cookbooks weren't meant as reading matter or novels as cookbooks, but I had replied that I got just as much pleasure and had just as many adventures reading Elizabeth David's *Italian Food* as *The Wind in the Willows*). Was I in a position not to care what the rest of the world thought of me? Sitting here with Humbert Coe, in the best restaurant in town, I wasn't yet able to say "yes" with as much confidence as I would have liked. I knew, with the unshakable certainty of a child, that my parents loved me, but because of my near invisibility outside the house I didn't know whether people appreciated me, or they loved me. Although I was never bullied at school I didn't have any real friends. And the fact that I was able to answer my teachers' most enigmatic questions, but not the most obvious ones, didn't make things any easier.

Our menus arrived. Coe leaned back in his chair, menu in his right hand, the index finger of the other pressed against his temple.

Barely two weeks after the start of my first year of secondary school I trod dangerously close to the edge of the abyss when, one day, I gave an oral report about truffle hunting in Umbria and, later that day in answer to our Dutch teacher, who had asked us to tell her our favorite book, had said mine was Xenophon's *Anabasis*. At recess, a group of my classmates began pushing me around. I had saved myself not by doing anything back, but by staring the boy who seemed to be the leader disdainfully in the eye. It hadn't been a conscious reaction. I didn't really know how to react. Just as I was about to lash out I saw, in embryo in the face of the boy opposite me, the features of a frightened little office clerk. That was the moment, I suddenly realized as I stared down at the menu and saw all those French names dancing before my eyes, that was the moment when I had suddenly felt strangely confident.

Coe put the menu aside and studied the wine list, nodding thoughtfully. Then he returned to the menu.

"It has always been my conviction that wine is the heart of the meal and that the rest of the meal must be built up around it. Do you drink wine?"

I nodded.

"Excellent. Then I suggest we start with a half bottle of gewürztraminer. I see here that they serve a rather old one. No doubt cellar remains, but that might well be to our advantage. An old Alsace, perhaps a bit past its prime, acquires a lovely golden color and a delightfully spicy taste with a trace of honey. After that . . ." He passed me the wine list and pointed to a column of names in which I could find the bottle he had in mind.

"After that I thought perhaps a Savigny-les-Beaunes. Out of curiosity, mainly. I wonder how it got on this list. It may have been a flash of insight, but it could equally well have been a fit of madness. Eh?"

I nodded again. I had drunk wine before, a festive glass on special occasions and sometimes, too, over the past few years, with a meal I had prepared, but I was certainly not the sophisticated drinker that Coe seemed to take me for. I had never drunk an Alsace and at the words Savigny-les-Beaunes I thought of old French nobility, the kind that had come down in the world because of exorbitant holidays in Cap d'Antibes and rash investments in Chilean copper mines.

Coe left the choice of dishes to me. I ordered, as an appetizer, a salad of breast of pigeon, lamb's lettuce, and walnuts, and for the entrée, lamb cutlets.

"Only *one* appetizer?"

I had made my choice out of politeness, but nevertheless nodded confidently. Coe pursed his lips.

The waiter took our orders and not long afterward the sommelier appeared with the bottle of gewürztraminer.

Up until the main course, the evening went quite well. I drank a glass of the Alsace that indeed proved to be a spicy, deep yellow wine, and in the meantime we ate our breast of pigeon and I looked around. The room was full of middle-aged couples staring silently at each other. At the back was a round table with five men who ordered one bottle of wine after another. Every now and then someone stole a glance at us, but that only made me feel more at ease. Coe did the talking, telling me about England, the military base where he and my father had spent some time together, but I didn't really seem to be hearing him. His words drifted across the table and dissolved in an overpowering feeling of contentment. Here I was and here was where I wanted to be. That night there wasn't a doubt in my mind.

When the main course arrived, my disappointment must have been obvious. Coe immediately leaned across the table and asked what was the matter. I pointed to the lamb cutlets, which were buried under a thick, grayish-brown sauce, and said, a touch of indignation in my voice, "I can't even see them."

My table companion nodded.

"And there are only two."

He kept on nodding.

I scraped off a bit of the sauce, found a cutlet, and tried to slice it.

"And they've been cooked too long. They're gray!"

Coe waited, with bated breath, for me to take my first bite.

I put the fork in my mouth and chewed. Fried cardboard in a sauce of ground egg cartons. I laid down my silverware and shifted my gaze from Coe to his plate. He smoothed his napkin and took a sample. His eyes stared over my head, at some vague point in the distance, his mouth slowly moving. When he had swallowed his mouthful, he, too, laid down his fork.

"It's perfectly clear," he said. "The poor creature has been slaughtered twice: once by the butcher and again, posthumously, by the chef. What do you think of the sauce?"

The waiter appeared and asked if everything was to our liking. Coe smiled. He gave me the kind of look that teachers give their best pupils and said, "My nephew is not entirely happy."

The waiter looked from Coe to me and from me to the swinging doors that led to the kitchen. "And what seems to be the trouble, sir?" he asked,

That was the wrong approach. I was willing to accept that some people didn't know how to cook, but if anyone treated me like a spoiled child who was just trying to be a nuisance, I got stubborn.

"Do you really want to know?" I asked.

"I'm burning with desire."

Coe looked around, grinning broadly. At several of the tables, the conversations flagged.

"The lamb cutlets are too well done. All you can

taste is the pan they were cooked in. They've been buried under a typical Dutch roux: lots of butter and flour and no taste. And I don't think the sauce was made *à la minute*."

The waiter looked at Coe. "The young man is quite the little connoisseur."

"The young man happens to be an excellent cook himself."

"Perhaps the young man's taste needs to develop a bit," said the waiter.

I smiled at him. "Would you like me to show the chef how it's done?"

The waiter turned on his heel and strode out of the dining room. Coe hooked his thumbs into his waistcoat and waited for what was to come.

From the back of the restaurant came the chef. He was still wearing his big hat and he looked as if he had just crawled out of a Dumpster. I didn't think that was a very good sign. Good cooks don't get dirty.

"Is there a problem?"

Coe nodded in my direction. I looked the chef straight in the eye and repeated what I had just said to the waiter.

"And you think you can do better?" He didn't sound unfriendly, just interested. I nodded.

"Well, then," he said. "Follow me. A bottle of wine

from me to you if a random customer likes your food better than mine."

"What kind of wine?"

The chef grinned. "Did you have one in mind?"

"There's an Haut Brion on the wine list."

Coe squinted and seemed to be thinking about something.

"And what's your bet?"

I got up from my chair. When we were standing face-to-face I came up to his armpits. His stomach stuck out so far that we had to stand several feet apart. "The same bottle," I said. The chef turned around and went ahead of me to the kitchen. "Are you sure you can afford it?" he asked over his shoulder. He pushed open the swinging doors and let me in. "Well?" I shook my head. "No," I said.

In the kitchen, on an empty space on the steel counter, I had him set before me a cup of cream (there was no crème fraîche), a cup of potato starch, and a dish of stock. I asked for a saucepan and poured in some of the stock. I placed the pan over a low flame, stirred the potato starch into the cream, and when the stock was warm enough I poured the cream into the pan. Several people had gathered around us: two boys my age, a man in a suit, and the waiter. "I need a small whisk." The chef nudged one of the boys. I was handed the whisk and I beat and stirred until the sauce was of the proper consistency. At my request I was brought thyme and a clove of garlic, which I crushed with the flat of a knife and added to the mixture on the stove, and then—I hadn't been busy for more than three or four minutes— I fished out the garlic and the sauce was ready.

"That's it?" the chef said.

I took the pan off the flame and nodded.

"Don't you have to heat it through?"

"No, that would weaken the flavor and make the sauce watery."

"Spoon!" yelled the chef.

One of the galley boys grabbed a spoon. The chef took some sauce and put it in his mouth. He closed his eyes. He tasted. He opened his eyes again. He looked at Coe, at me, and then at his apprentice. "Make a note," he said. "You there!" He shouted to a waiter. "You got a lamb cutlet on order?" The waiter shook his head, "Too late, we just served it." The chef pulled open the refrigerator and slapped two curling pieces of lamb down on the stainless steel countertop. He looked at me. "It's all yours," he said. And to the waiter, "Bring it back. There's another one coming."

I switched to another burner and cooked the cutlets *au point*, the way I had learned from the many books I had read over the years. I was slightly nervous—the kitchen was unfamiliar, the equipment was different, and I had never done lamb cutlets before—but I knew I could rely on my intuition. That was something I had discovered over the last few years. I could analyze a dish without tasting it, I could cook without measuring, and I could prepare any dish after only one reading of a recipe that described something similar. It wasn't a talent, as Coe had said to my father earlier. It was intuition, imagination, or perhaps it was a talent after all, the talent to abstract a thing as organic and chaotic as cooking. When I was finished, the plate went out the door and Coe rested his hand on my shoulder. His round face was reflected in the gleaming metal of the rear wall of the stove. His eyebrows, which seemed to wriggle above his black eyes like caterpillars, gave him the appearance of a gluttonous Benedictine. He began to lecture the chef on what he called a "leveling of taste," that dishes nowadays often had a kind of "surface taste" which could no longer be broken down into its various components. "Dutch chefs," he said, "are afraid to let us taste the ingredients that compose a dish. When I eat hare, I want to taste hare, wine, thyme, and scallions, not some all-purpose herb mix."

The waiter came back into the kitchen. He looked like an undertaker.

"Well?" asked the man in the suit.

"He asked what the hell was going on."

I suddenly noticed how hot it was in the kitchen.

"What did he mean?" asked the chef.

"He said, 'Is this some kind of test, first I get served that greasy dreck and then I get the real dish?' "

I avoided looking at the chef, who had raised his head and was staring at something at the back of the kitchen.

"Well well," he said.

"What's dreck?" asked the waiter.

The chef began smiling.

A waitress came in and after two steps shrank back in alarm.

"What's up, Thea?"

She stood next to the swinging doors and looked suspiciously at the little group around the stove. "There's nothing coming through," she said. "Table Eight's been waiting half an hour for two *dames blanches*."

I shivered.

"Bet you can do that better too, huh?" said the chef. He signaled to one of his galley boys, who got out the ice cream and started preparing the desserts. The waiter, who still didn't know what dreck was, left the kitchen.

"You've earned that Haut Brion," said the chef. "What do you say we open it right now?"

I thought that was a fine idea.

"The sauce," he said. "That was your recipe?"

"It's based on a couple of things from Artusi."

Coe leaned toward me slightly. "You've read Artusi?"

One of the galley boys came in with the wine. He handed it to his boss, who carefully uncorked it and put it down on the wooden table in the middle of the kitchen. There was bread, cheese, salt, and water. The chef poured me a finger of wine. I swirled it in my glass, sniffed, took a sip, sloshed it around a bit, and then nodded.

"Dear boy," said Coe, "who taught you this great love of food?"

"I did, I think. And Mrs. David."

"Mrs. Who?" said the chef.

"Elizabeth David," said Coe. "That, De Jong, is your problem: you don't keep up with the literature. An Englishwoman, who writes primarily on French and Italian cuisine. How else do you think this young lad, in this poor country, would have heard of garlic and crème fraîche?"

I looked at Coe and took a sip of the fragrant Haut Brion. I had never tasted this wine before. I had seen it mentioned in a wine guide I'd read in the bookstore. The description had been so enthusiastic that I had never forgotten the name.

"I don't think you're a cook at all." Coe said, turning to me, "Cooking isn't even particularly interesting. A cook is always having to contend with limitations: the kitchen, the boss, the customers, the region, the country. If you can you should write about food."

"If everybody wrote about food and nobody cooked anymore, Campbell's soup would be the Bocuse of everyday life," said the chef irritably.

Coe drank his wine. He smacked his lips and then pursed them. "An excellent choice. What would you have liked to eat with this?"

"Tagliatelle with ragout of lamb and maybe a salad: curly endive and sweet potato."

The chef frowned. "Sweet potato?" he mumbled.

Coe looked at me in surprise. He thought for a moment. Then he nodded slowly. "I think," he said, "we'll have to do this more often."

That night when I came home, my mother was sitting at the table, reading. She kissed me, and recoiled in horror. "You've been drinking!" I smiled like a tailor who has sewn himself into his own suit. "An Haut Brion," I said. "I won it cooking." She shook her head and stood up. As we walked upstairs, I told her about my peculiar dinner with Coe and my heroic feats in Lejeune's kitchen. In the bathroom, I brushed my teeth, while she looked at me in the mirror. "Promise me one thing," she said. "Whatever happens, you'll finish school." I laughed too loudly and nodded. "I mean it," she said. "Boris had to do it all later, and he's never really amounted to anything." I rinsed my mouth, and as I spit the water into the sink, where the red of the wine and the white of the toothpaste formed a dirty gray foam, I suddenly felt an ominous kind of sadness creeping up inside me.

Three

EVEN THOUGH IT DIDN'T STOP RAINING, MY MOTHER
and I went that summer, like every other summer, to the
village in the dunes where her father had been mayor.
He now spent his days polishing his old rifles, waiting
for friends who, like him, had come to look more and
more like shuffling old badgers. His wife wandered
through the house with a wicker basket, in which she
carried a bunch of keys and a cologne-soaked handkerchief. Her life was an endless opening and closing of
doors, restless peering into empty rooms, and whis-
pered mumbling. Ever since she had asked the baker for
half a loaf of green and a loaf of plaid, sliced, they had
had a housekeeper.

Those two weeks in the dunes had never been an
excursion I'd particularly looked forward to. Even
before she had gotten lost in the fog my grandmother
had looked at me sideways, and my grandfather, for as
long as I could remember, seemed to be awaiting the
moment when I would prove myself a man, grab one
of his old rifles, and shoot a prizewinning rabbit. Now

that it wouldn't stop raining, that annual visit was even less appealing. The bad weather however only seemed to increase my mother's determination. According to her, it was usually better at the seaside, and the salty air would do me good.

A day after our arrival, my grandfather called me into what he referred to as his "study." I hardly ever entered that room. It was at the back of the house and overlooked a rolling stretch of dunes covered with tough, sharp grass. In the distance you could see the first houses of the village he had governed half his life without much enthusiasm and where he now, in more ways than one, was an outsider. The walls were hung with tinted etchings of hunters riding horses frozen in a ludicrous swan dive. Here and there was a rifle leaning against the bookcase, and the smell of grease and gun oil was so overpowering that it could just as easily have been a gunsmith's workshop.

My grandfather pointed me to a chair that came from the old council chamber, on the back of which was the faded, embroidered coat of arms of the village, a plump little fish that floated, grinning stupidly, above something that looked like the serrated blade of a knife, but was no doubt meant to represent the sea. "I've asked you here . . ." He cleared his throat, removed a book of illustrations of lushly colored pheasants from his chair, and lowered himself down. "I've asked you here, because you . . . well, because you're nearly grown, a grown man, and it seemed to me that it was time we talked man . . . to man." He looked visibly relieved to have the introduction over and done with. I wouldn't have been surprised if he had stood up, shaken my hand, and shown me to the door.

But he sat back, let his fingertips wander over the arm of the chair and, for a moment, seemed very far away. Then he straightened up again. "You're not a hunter," he said. His head came up slowly, until he was looking me straight in the eye. His expression was accusatory and shy at the same time. I felt the urge to say that I *was* a hunter, that I would like nothing better than to march into the dunes with one of his rifles and kill something. "Your father wasn't a hunter, either." I realized that he meant something different than I had thought. "I had a word with my good friend Van der Molen last week." That was the old lawyer, one of the men he played bridge with, chased small game with. "I've made my will." He was looking at me closely now. "A will is a . . ." I nodded. "You know. All right. I have set up a fund whose goal is to buy up this land, piece by piece." He gestured vaguely behind him, to where the dunes lay. "In due course, all that will become a shooting ground. This house will be the office and the home of the proprietor, the director." He paused. "You will be the director." He fell silent. Outside was a whispering rain, above us was the sound of footsteps on wooden floors.

"The director?"

"Yes." He sprang to his feet, unexpectedly buoyant, rubbed his hands together, and began pacing to and fro. "The director! Imagine!" He ran his eyes over the walls, over the colored etchings, the dented bugle that a long-forgotten prince consort had flung to the ground, after an unsuccessful hunting party, during which they had hit only rabbits and hares, and left behind. He raised his right arm, his hand on a level with his face, and said, "One day. All this. Will be yours."

I suddenly saw myself standing in front of the house in a kind of red-and-green elf costume, watching a troop of exuberant hunters on horseback as they disappeared into the dunes to slay a dragon.

"I'm only twelve," I said.

"Nonsense!" He thrust out his chin. "A man's character is formed in his early youth. At your age, in fact. Playtime is over. Port?"

I was in no shape to answer. My grandfather walked over to a low cabinet, on top of which was a silver tray with bottles and decanters, and filled two glasses with syrupy, reddish-brown liquid. He handed one to me and then, sipping from his own glass, resumed his pacing. "A man has got to make something of himself. Some men go to college, some work their way up, others need a guiding hand . . ." He clenched his fist and held it out in front of him, as if he thought it was important that I saw it. ". . . the guiding hand of an experienced older man."

My eyes followed him back and forth, back and forth. I wanted to tear myself away from this mad conversation, from his self-absorbed pacing, but I couldn't. I was mesmerized by the bizarre flight his thoughts had taken.

"That was what your father lacked. Because of the war, many young men were hurled into the thick of it. Left to their own devices. Without law and order. Without the . . . the soothing effect of civilization." He was on my side of the room now and stopped right in front of me. He peered into my eyes from under his bushy eyebrows. "Drink your port."

I wrenched myself away from him, raised my glass, and poured it down my throat. A sudden warmth exploded in my chest, shot up to my head, and filled my ears. My grandfather turned around like an old tortoise and started back toward the other end of the room. I waited, my eyes wide open, for the fire in my throat to die.

Outside, a storm had come up. The wind tugged at the young trees along the path to the beach and the clouds blew across the village like shreds of unwashed curtain. My grandfather's voice came from far away. He was holding forth about civilization and "the Huns" (whoever they were), about the hunt . . . Slowly I began to lose the thread of his story. The warmth of the port had nestled in my stomach and feet and the chair had become soft and embracing. I closed my eyes and saw myself standing in the doorway of the house again, in a green jerkin and a little red jacket, while Robin Hood's Merry Men armed themselves with bows and arrows and set off for the dunes. I remember thinking that this wasn't quite what my grandfather had had in mind when he had told me about his plans for a hunting reserve. After that I must have fallen asleep, because when I opened my eyes again, the windows were black and the room was empty.

OUR VISIT LASTED ten days, but I can't say I remember much of it. Most mornings I'd wriggle my way into a pair of Wellington boots and head for the dunes. There I'd sit, on the roof of a bunker that was half buried in the sand, gazing out at the gray sea. The sky was dead and dreary, like the sea, and the sand was wet and dark and it felt as if the whole world were sitting by roaring fires in warm, comfortable living rooms, waiting for the next storm. Sometimes my mother would come with me and then the two of us would sit there in silence, gazing out at the slow raging of the surf. One afternoon, when we were looking out at that pencil-sketched world from the roof of the bunker, she fished a pack of cigarettes from her jacket pocket and took out a Lucky. She had a hard time getting it lit. I watched her and waited for her to speak, but she said nothing. The smoke blew in her eyes. After a while, she dropped the cigarette in the damp sand and shook her head. I peered into the endlessly rolling waves. The wind tugged at my hood.

On one of those rare afternoons when the sky cleared up briefly, I went looking for my mother to ask her to come with me to the bunker, but I couldn't find her. I did run into my grandmother though. She was standing in a hallway, muttering angrily at a portrait of a gentleman with a pince-nez and a high collar. As I passed her she nodded her head toward the dream room. I looked at her for a moment, dumbfounded, but she turned and shuffled away to the staircase.

My mother was sitting with her knees raised on the wide sill of the bay window. The light of the sun, which had already gone down behind the dunes, shimmered softly on her skin. The sea glistened in the distance and the wet sand, just beginning to dry, had an iridescent sheen. My mother's head was raised slightly and she was staring out the window. She must have been cold, because she had her arms wrapped around her and was hugging them tightly.

By the time she noticed my presence, I was already standing next to her. She didn't look at me when she said my name.

"I used to sit here and read."

I looked out the curved window.

She turned her head toward me.

I frowned. Her eyes were large and dark. We looked at each other for a while and then suddenly she reached out her arm and pulled me toward her, my face in her waist. She smelled like grass.

"Would you like me to read to you?" Her voice sounded faint.

I shook my head.

"Do you think that you are too old for that kind of thing?"

I tried to shrug my shoulders. She let me go. I leaned against her hip and said, "I came to ask if you wanted to go to the bunker."

Her gaze wandered, to the sea, the raw sky above it that, even now, was threatening a storm that would drive away this clarity. "Let's wait. I want to walk in the rain. We'll put on our windbreakers and boots and go outside."

I laughed, a bit incredulously.

"What, you think I'm getting as funny as your grandmother?"

"She was standing in the hallway, talking to a photograph."

My mother climbed out of the window seat and stretched her arms. Her back hollowed, her face was turned to the ceiling. "Why on earth do we ever come here?" she said. "This must be the most boring place in the world."

She was acting strange this afternoon. She was saying things she didn't normally say.

She ruffled my hair with her fingertips, which made it stick straight up, and then walked around the room, her hands clasped behind her back, with odd little ballerina steps. She peered up at the framed photographs on the walls. Each photo, each print—some had been cut out of magazines, others came from markets and bazaars—had a special meaning. Above the wide wooden bed hung a photograph of a path that disappeared into a dark, tangled forest. There were other pictures, hung at varying heights, showing elaborate picnics held long ago under shady trees, empty bottles here and there, baskets of strawberries and peaches.

There were photographs of boat races with lots of flags and cheering spectators, and a reproduction of a page from a medieval book of hours, in which one group of travelers toiled up a winding mountain path while another group strolled down a wide dirt road from one jolly inn to the next.

WHEN MY FATHER was moved from the hospital to the village in the dunes, he had had a relapse. That afternoon he was running a fever and felt too weak to get out of bed. The doctor, who happened to be there anyway—he was just about to go off hunting with my grandfather—quickly examined the patient and said that it was "the exertion of the journey," nothing to worry about. He advised rest, plenty of fresh fruit and fresh air. When he was gone, leaving behind the smell of boot wax and gun oil, the young nurse sat at her patient's bedside, musing. She looked at the patient, lying there on his pillow in a troubled sleep. His forehead was beaded with droplets of sweat, his parched lips seemed to be searching for something. The exertion of the journey? Nothing to worry about? She wasn't so sure.

She tried to imagine how he must feel, feverish, in unfamiliar surroundings, anxious, perhaps, about his future. A fallen angel. He had liked it when she read to him. "I hear your voice," he had said, "and I close my eyes and see what you're telling me. Sometimes the story goes left, but I go right."

That afternoon she climbed the stairs to the attic, armed with a flashlight and the decisiveness of someone who didn't plan to seek, but was certain she would find. She didn't know when anyone had been up in the attic last. Her father never went up there, why should he? She wasn't sure about her mother, but she couldn't really imagine her moving around in this dark, dusty space in one of her voluminous black dresses.

When she got upstairs she saw that she was right. The last additions to the attic were standing, any which way, around the stairwell. Someone, her mother or perhaps the maid, had lugged everything up the stairs and dumped it on the first available bit of floor space, then fled. She shone her flashlight over the dusty boxes and piles. Right next to the stairwell stood a crate that had once contained wine and now turned out to be full of commemorative plates, flags and pennons, and hideous tin beakers. She held a plate up to her flashlight and read the words around the rim. The pseudo-medieval handwriting was hard to decipher, but it wasn't long before she figured out that it was a souvenir of the mayor's visit to a Belgian city. The rest was more of the same: a shield commemorating the fifth anniversary of a

friendly alliance between her father's village and that of
a French mayor, whom she suddenly remembered as
the "Uncle Gaston" who had had the annoying habit of
grabbing her hands and rubbing them along his badly
shaven cheeks; an embroidered standard made by the
local chapter of the Christian Housewives' Association
on the occasion of the Queen's silver wedding anniversary; the dusty, moth-eaten head of a wild boar that,
according to the inscription on a small metal plaque, had
been shot on October 3, 1929, in the Black Forest. She
pushed the crate out of the way and shone her flashlight
over the dark walls. The attic extended over the length
and breadth of the house and was divided into a large
central area, where the stairs emerged, and four tiny
rooms, on the left and right, that had once been the servants' quarters. As a child she had always wanted to
play up here, but her mother, probably because she herself didn't dare go upstairs, wouldn't allow it.

When she returned downstairs that afternoon she
was carrying a burlap bag over her shoulder that was so
heavy she had to stop and rest halfway down the stairs.
Back in the room of her patient, who had fallen into a
deep sleep and whose face had an unpleasantly waxen
serenity about it, she began distributing her loot over
the walls. The two items still hanging there—a funereal
painting of the moors and a calendar that had last been

torn off in February 1937, with a faded illustration of a small Romanesque chapel in the north of the country— she laid on the top shelf of a closet. Even though she had to hammer in a nail here and there, the sick man didn't wake up.

At the end of the day, when my father finally opened his eyes, the sun was shining so low that he seemed to float in soft orange light. His eyes fell on a group of men in straw hats with striped bands, clutching an enormous oar. In the background the shady water of a tree-lined rowing course sparkled, little flags hung from the trees and boats lay keel-side-down in the grass. He had seen a boating race once, in England, and now his thoughts turned back to that afternoon. The scent of freshly mown grass rose in his nostrils, he could smell the dark water. Ice tinkled in glasses and a woman's high laughter drifted up to the treetops. Then he dropped off to sleep again.

As it turned out, it wasn't the journey that had caused my father's relapse, nor any other type of exertion, but an infection in an old wound. A course of penicillin, for which my mother jabbed a sturdy needle in his buttock twice a day, soon had him back on his feet, although my mother, with the same obstinacy with which she had once christened him Boris, would always insist that it was the paintings and photographs that had cured him.

The same painting that still hung in the sunny room that she now referred to as the dream room. I turned around and looked out at the sea, the light above the water, which cast a dirty green haze over the waves.

"It's going to start pouring any minute," I said.

My mother came and stood next to me. "Maybe it'll be raining too hard to go outside."

My face clouded over.

"But who cares! Quick, get your windbreaker. Put on your boots. We're off!"

We ran out of the room, grabbed our jackets from the coat rack, and shot out the door before anyone could say anything sensible. We ran down the brick path to the gap in the dunes that opened onto the beach and felt the rising breeze. When we reached the foot of the dunes the wind came rushing toward us like an old friend. We backed away, grabbing each other by the sleeve. The tide was still going out. The wet strip of sand along the water was a cluttered trail of driftwood, seaweed, and dead fish. The sky was dark gray with a sickly purplish hue. We walked about a quarter of an hour along the tidemark, kicking at the flotsam and jetsam with the toes of our boots, and then turned back. As we reached the bunker, the clouds burst and the rain came down in such thick drops that we had to stop walking, because we suddenly couldn't see a thing.

Then we ran into the dune, slipped through the hole in the bunker, and sat there, crouched, our backs against the damp concrete.

The rain fell the way it had been falling for weeks: as if melting glass was streaming from the heavens. My mother rummaged around in the pocket of her jacket and took out her cigarettes. The narrow entrance to the bunker began to smell spicily of Luckies. I followed a shred of smoke as it drifted outside and disappeared in the pouring rain. In the distance, barely visible in the roaring flood of rain, someone was walking. He came down the brick path, half stooped, shoulders hunched. He was wearing a long coat that he held closed at the neck with his right hand. Not far from the bunker, he came to a halt. Shielding his eyes with his hand, he looked first left, then right. The entrance to the bunker was dark and the rain made it even harder to see. His eyes skimmed over the dunes, the bunker, the gap between the dunes, the sea. Then he pulled his collar tighter around him and walked onto the beach.

Next to me, my mother threw the rest of her cigarette in the sand and slowly got to her feet. "Come on," she said. "Let's give it a try." As we were getting up, we suddenly heard a plaintive sound, like a baby crying. My mother raised her head. She took a step in the direction of where she thought the sound was coming from, turned back again—and then stood there like a watchful animal, head raised and tilted, listening. After a while she went farther into the bunker. Leaning forward, still halfway in the dark entrance, she lit a match.

"Smoking has its advantages," she said.

Against the back wall, where it stank of filthy toilets and wet sand, lay a cat. My mother threw away the match, handed me the box, and asked me to light another one.

"I thought it was a child," I said, as we looked at the cat in the restless light of the flame.

My mother squatted down next to the animal and examined it with the skill of a nurse. "Cats can sound frighteningly human," she said. She felt its flanks with her right hand, while stroking the head with her left. I threw the match on the ground and lit another.

"We'll stay here a while and wait. It won't take long."

"What won't?"

"She's having kittens."

I recoiled. "I'll wait outside."

She looked at me over her shoulder and raised one eyebrow. "No you won't. I'll need you to light another match for me soon. And I want you to see this."

"But I don't want to see it!" I flung the match to the ground and shuffled my feet.

"You can't avoid everything. We're staying here."

The cat had stopped howling. We, too, fell silent, in the muffled hush of the bunker. It was very dark and it was a long time before we were able to see something.

Nearly an hour passed before we left the bunker. In the meantime, the cat had four kittens, blind little worms that burrowed their noses into their mother's belly. When we came outside, it had stopped raining. Tattered gray clouds scudded over the water, toward the shore, and except for one lonely figure at the tidemark, the beach was deserted. My mother was just turning around, toward the house, when I caught sight of the figure. I peered into the wind, my eyes watering, and didn't hear my mother calling until she had come back to get me.

"Didn't you hear? I . . ."

I didn't look at her, but saw her hand go to her mouth.

"But that's . . ."

There at the tidemark, massive and tall, his coattails flapping, staring at the raging sea, stood Humbert Coe.

THAT EVENING WE ATE in the parlor, by the light of a candelabra I had seen gathering dust on a sideboard for as long as I could remember. The candle flames swayed gently in the twilight and cast a feverish glow on the faces of my mother and Humbert Coe. A bottle had been brought up from the cellar that made Coe nod with approval. He had poured it with his large hands into a crystal decanter that was new to me.

It was a while before I realized that I hadn't seen my grandparents for quite a while. When I asked about them, I was told that they had eaten upstairs.

I hadn't exactly been looking forward to an interminable meal with my gun-and-rabbit-crazy grandfather and my vacantly staring grandmother, but the fact that they weren't there, in their own house, seemed odd to me. I didn't get the chance to pursue the matter. My mother firmly evaded my glances and launched into deep conversation with Coe.

The room was at the front of the house, where the large bay window provided a clear view of the rolling dunes and the great void of sea and sky. Now, in the darkness, you could see only the faint, distant light of the moon through shreds of cloud and the reflection of the flickering candles on the windowpane. A few hours earlier Coe had sat here, a towel draped across his shoulders, his hair still somewhat wet and wild. He drank from a cup that looked so small in those big hands that I would have found it perfectly normal if he had grabbed the whole teapot and drunk straight from the spout. There were still raindrops leaking from his hair and every now and then he gave a thunderous sneeze and shivered from head to toe.

It was soon decided that Coe would spend the night at my grandparents' house. There weren't many trains running at night, and besides, he was chilled to the bone. Even though he himself mumbled "taxi," and that he'd be fine, really, my mother had brushed aside his objections with her usual briskness and asked the housekeeper to make up a bed in the dream room. I had thrown her a bemused look that she chose to ignore. Instead she sent me into the kitchen to see what we could serve for dinner that night. The cellar and pantry were well stocked, and there was a hare hanging in the scullery that the doctor had brought over two days before. When my mother came in an hour later to see where I was, the potatoes had already been peeled and the hare lay browning in a roasting tin. I was sitting on a kitchen chair, in the hot, heady scent of dried prunes simmering in wine, and stared at the drops of condensation rolling down the kitchen window.

"What are you making?"

I told her. She looked at me with a mixture of surprise and uneasiness. "I thought you weren't allowed to shoot hare in the summertime," she said. I grinned. She smiled wearily. "Did you skin that beast yourself?" I nodded. A barely perceptible shiver went through her. Once, when she was still very young, Grandfather had taught her how to skin a hare and pluck a pheasant. It was not a success. For several years afterward, she had been a vegetarian.

She disappeared into the cellar and after a while came back with two bottles. She put them on the table and looked at me expectantly. I nodded, she sat down across from me at the table and let her eyes drift around the room. "Do you think we should come and live here some day?" I shrugged. "I don't think Boris would like it much," I said. She shook her head. I had the vague feeling that she wanted to tell me something or wanted me to say something to her, but I had no idea what. "Well," she said, "I'll bring the wine into the other room."

She was already at the door to the hallway when I called her name. She looked back over her shoulder, bottles in her arms, wisps of hair around her face. She looked much younger than she really was. Her cheeks were flushed and the light from the lamp glittered in her eyes.

"How did he end up here, do you think?"

She looked at me for a while. "Coe?" she said. She shrugged her shoulders, pushed open the door with her foot, and walked on.

Halfway through the evening—the hare a jumble of bones, the foggy glasses, and the decanter nearly empty—there was a flash of lightning above the sea. It flickered blue between the clouds and you could hear a distant rumbling of thunder. We looked outside. Coe wondered why a thunderstorm at sea was always so different than inland, and my mother remembered how, in her youth, lightning had struck in the village. Just then the door opened and the black-clad figure of my grandmother appeared. She stood in the doorway with the cologne-soaked handkerchief over her mouth and stared, wide-eyed, at the candlelit scene.

"Julia!" she said. "The parachute!"

My mother shot out of her chair. Her glass fell. A red stain began spreading over the tablecloth.

"Mama," she cried.

"Ma'am," said Coe. He got to his feet, his left hand on his chest. "My sincerest apologies. It was never my intention to . . . blow in here . . . so unannounced."

"The parachute!" cried my grandmother again. "Julia, you've got to hide the parachute!"

"The weather," said Coe. "Took me by surprise. Terrible storm."

I stared at him in amazement.

My mother laid her hand on her mother's shoulder. "Everything's been taken care of, Mama."

My grandmother stared a few seconds more at the visitor and then allowed my mother to lead her out of the room.

"My mother has hardening of the arteries," she said, when she returned. "She's very confused." She raised her glass and only noticed that it was empty when she was about to take a sip. I stood up and poured her another drink. She took a large gulp, nearly choked, and dabbed at her lips with the napkin. When her eyes fell on the wine stain on the tablecloth, she jerked her head away.

There was a lengthy silence, during which I tried to figure out what was going on. Things somehow weren't what they ought to be. I couldn't put it into words, but it reminded me of a doubly exposed photograph, in which you saw two images: one real, and the other a faint echo of the first.

As I sat there brooding, I felt my eyes growing heavy. The walk on the beach, the glass of wine, and the steady swaying of the candle flames were beginning to take effect. It wasn't long before my mother saw my head nodding and sent me upstairs. I protested feebly, but there wasn't any point. She wouldn't be contradicted and I was too tired to offer much resistance. I shook Coe's hand and kissed my mother and headed for my room.

When I got upstairs I was just barely able to lay my clothes on the back of a chair. I must have fallen asleep the moment my head hit the pillow.

THAT NIGHT I WAS AWAKENED by the slamming of the front door. It was nearly midnight, I had slept less than two hours, but I sat bolt upright in bed and was wide awake. I went to the window and looked outside, where, as I had expected, there was nothing to see. Without knowing why and without thinking, I threw on my clothes and sneaked out the door. On the stairs, I could feel a clammy chill moving through the house. The front door stood wide open and with every gust of wind it banged against the doorframe. The latch had been pulled out, so it couldn't fall shut. Coe's and my mother's coats were missing from the coatrack. I pulled on my jacket and boots and walked to the door. Then I suddenly remembered my grandfather's flashlight and I ran to his room to get it.

When I came back into the hallway, my grandmother was standing on the stairs. Her long gray hair hung down over the shawl she wore over her white nightgown and for a moment she looked like the ghost of my mother.

"The parachute," I said. It was the first thing that

came to my mind. I'd barely uttered the words, when all of a sudden I began to understand. The doubly exposed picture I'd thought of before became clear: one of the images, the most recent one, dissolved and what was left, a still life from the past, came into focus.

"I have to go bury the parachute."

My grandmother pulled the shawl tighter around her and nodded, relieved.

"Go back to sleep. I'll take care of everything."

She turned around and walked back up the stairs. I waited until the white of her nightgown was smothered by the darkness and I had heard the click of her bedroom door.

Outside in the cone of light from my flashlight I saw puddles and small meandering streams that barely hid a crisscross of footprints that seemed to lead to the beach. The rain was pouring down so hard that I couldn't keep my eyes open unless I bowed my head. But I knew these surroundings like the back of my hand, and even in the darkness and the rain I had no trouble finding my way to the beach.

There must have been a moon hiding behind the clouds, but it wasn't much use to me. Now and then a thin patch slipped past in the blanket of clouds and a stain appeared in the sky, but that stain never grew to be more than a vague suggestion of moonlight. And so it was dark and wet and wet and dark.

My first guess was the bunker, since that was the only dry place for miles around, but there was no one there. Even the mother cat and her kittens had disappeared. I shone my flashlight over the gray walls, the obscene drawings and carvings that, in the glow of the flashlight, suddenly looked prehistoric.

When I left the bunker, my back bent, my head bowed, a pair of shoes appeared in the glow of the flashlight. My fear lasted only a moment. I didn't need to raise my head or shine upward. I knew who belonged to those feet.

Wet and windblown, the collar of his coat held together with both hands and his hair plastered around his face, was my father. He looked at me, shook his head, and then motioned toward the bunker.

When we were crouched down across from each other, our backs to the wall, the flashlight like a cold campfire between the bottles and cigarette butts on the ground, he pulled a pack of cigarettes out of his coat pocket, fished out a rain-soaked Lucky, and lit it. The cigarette went out after two puffs. He looked at it for a moment and then tossed it away.

"What," he said, "is going on here?"

I took a deep breath and began telling him what had happened in the last few hours, how we had found Coe on the beach, that I had skinned and roasted a hare, that we had eaten, and how, later that night, I had been woken up by the front door blowing open and shut. I said nothing about the parachute or my grandmother.

My father listened silently and when I'd finished, told me that he had arrived on the last train, got lost in the rain, warmed up in a café with coffee and a glass of cognac, and finally, around midnight, had arrived at my grandparents' house. The door stood open. There was no one downstairs, my mother's room was empty and the bed unslept in, I was sound asleep. So he had gone back outside, in search. Seeing as how he didn't know the surroundings as well as I did, he had wandered around for a long time in the wet darkness before ending up at the bunker.

We sat opposite each other and stared at the wet sand between us. My father seemed to be thinking. The thumb and middle finger of his left hand massaged his temples and his eyes were closed.

"You go back," he said after a while, "I'll keep looking."

I didn't think that was a very good idea. Two would see more than one, and I knew the dunes far better than he did. Besides, I was wide awake and could never fall back to sleep knowing that my entire family was roaming around, through wind and rain, in the dead of night. My father nodded thoughtfully. Then he shook his head and beckoned.

It's funny how you can always see the surf, even on a rainy night. The crests of the waves, when we got to the beach, looked like pale ghosts trying to escape from a hellish darkness, and you could clearly hear, even in the pouring rain, their deep, muffled groans. My father's hand lay on my left shoulder and every now and then, as we walked along the tidemark, he steered me so that the beams of the flashlight fell here, then there.

We plodded left, so that we would be walking against the wind and rain, and walked half an hour without seeing anything but sand and water and darkness. Then, when we could just make out the lighthouse at the mouth of the harbor, we slowed down and turned our backs to the wind. My father drew his hand through his wet hair, brushing it out of his eyes.

"Why don't we walk back through the dunes?" I yelled against the wind. "We'll be sheltered from the rain, and it'll give us a chance to look around there."

But the dunes weren't much better than the beach. We had a hard time finding the path, and once we did, the sand was so soft and wet that it was another hour before we spotted the bunker. I shone my flashlight, which was growing steadily weaker, inside, and then we headed back for the house.

Downstairs, in the sun lounge, the lights were on. The glow from the windows beckoned to us, and suddenly I felt how cold and wet and tired I was. I shivered in my windbreaker. My face was numb and my legs were so wet that my trousers chafed my skin. We went up to the windows and saw Coe sitting in an armchair, slumped, his head hung low. My mother sat in front of him on the ground, her hair loose and dark with rain. For a minute, maybe less, we looked at this strange tableau. Then my father raised his hand and tapped on the glass.

Four

SOMETIMES A CHILD—ELBOWS ON THE WORKBENCH, chin cupped in his or her hands, eyes locked on the ball—asks me if "it" is for sale.

"It," I say, "it is mine."

Nine boys and two girls, all of them of exotic ethnic descent, all of them speak the kind of hip urban lingo that keeps reminding me of rusty barbed wire. Eleven faces that look up and wait for me to tell The Story, the story of How It Was and How It Began. It. I pick it up, weigh it, and feign deep thoughts that have drifted off, far away, long ago, a different world, when we were good and the summers long and hot. Sticky tubes of glue are being dropped, brushes laid aside. Mouths open, eyes glaze over. Behind those eleven faces an eyebrow curves in a woman's face: an immaculate little black comma over a large almond-shaped eye.

"Long ago," I say, as I sample the gathering. "Very long ago, when you weren't born yet . . ."

"When we still lived in Morocco," yells one.

"Turkey!" yells another.

"Pa. Ra. Ma. Ri. Bo!" roars yet another one.

"Somalia," whispers number four.

I raise my hand. "A long time ago indeed, very long ago, there was a man who could fly."

There is a skeptical quality in Nur's brow that spills into her eyes. She lifts her glass and blows on her tea, quite aware of the effect it has on me.

One moment of speechlessness. Then I shiver and speak.

It all started with one little boy who came to the shop and, looking around and noticing the sand-colored Dakota, asked if it was for sale, finished that is. I looked him over, got the smallest box from the shelves, ripped the shrink-wrap with my nail, and got the little bag out. "Look," I said. "That's it. Twenty, thirty parts. It'll take about an hour. Perhaps you can find someone to help you." His face told me that there was no one.

The neighborhood has changed. The families of old, with their 2.3 children and the steaming pot of tea that waits after school, have disappeared. Twenty years ago you'd see blue-haired little old ladies in knitted suits doing their shopping. Now it's Turks, Moroccans, Cape Verdeans, Hindustani, Chinese, and God knows where they all come from. And there are the single mothers, and fathers. The sort of families, anyway, that don't have the time to indulge in good and wholesome handiwork. The shoe shops with their beige old ladies' shoes have been replaced by twenty-four-hour Chinese restaurants, Islamic butchers, and Moroccan bakers. And where once the faint smell of office stationers lingered, with their dusty displays of pencils and faded notebooks, now one would smell fresh coriander, the heavy sweetness of Turkish pastry, and the red-hot kitchens of The Great Wall and Asian Glories.

That was what I was thinking of, the neighborhood and how it, and I, had grown and changed, and I looked at the boy and suddenly told him to return next Wednesday. I would try to round up a few more kids and we would build together. He shot me a look that was at the same time incredulous and surprised. Only after he'd left, while I was cutting a mold on the workbench, did I realize what I had done. I put the knife down and stared at the kites that hung from the ceiling, the sewing machine and the fluorescent yellow thread that ran through the needle, the spools, neatly lined up, the rolls of fabric along the wall, and I thought: the time has gone when a man could invite a couple of kids from the neighborhood for a glass of lemonade and some wholesome handiwork without getting his face in the papers. "Who the hell do you think you are?" I yelled into the empty space. "Baden-Powell?"

But my initial hesitation didn't save me and now they're here: eleven children, their mouths open, sitting around a workbench that's cluttered with shears, Stanley knives, pieces of nylon fabric, and loose threads. They're fingering glasses of Coke now, the silence for the first time since they came in so complete that it's almost audible.

I've told that story before, the one about the man who could fly. The boy who picked up the sphere has reached out before to touch the thick glass. It doesn't seem to matter. It's not the story; it's the way it's told.

"A sculptor and his son were imprisoned on an island," I say, "where the sculptor had to work for the king. The king had everything he desired. Gold overflowed his treasure chamber, a hundred beautiful girls with hair as black as the night and faces like the full moon served him at his table, dressed him in the morning, and entertained him as they danced in the evening in front of the fire in the great hall, and every night fifty strong men painted a new sky on the ceiling and fresh trees on the pillars, so that it seemed as if the clouds moved and the trees grew. One thing was missing: a wife. The king could have taken any of the beautiful girls for a wife, of course, and all of them would probably have been more than happy to be chosen, but the king wanted beauty to surpass anything he'd ever seen, and as he saw the hundred beautiful girls every day,

dancing and singing and serving him, none of them
would do. That is why he had called for a sculptor, to
make a statue of the fairest woman in the world. At first
the sculptor felt very honored, but after one of the girls
had told him what the king had in mind, he'd started
thinking of ways to escape. 'Dear sculptor,' the girl had
said, 'you must know that the king is a mighty sorcerer
who wants to bring your statue to life to marry her. No
one in the world must know, and so he will kill you after
you're finished.' That frightened the sculptor. Not
because he feared death—he was old and famous and
life had been good to him—but he had brought his son
with him to the island, to work as his assistant, and the
boy was just thirteen. And then there was something
else. After he'd been chiseling the huge block of marble
for a few weeks, he had discovered that it was not just a
statue he was sculpting. One night he had entered the
studio and the light of the moon, which came from far
away, over the sea, was soft and blue. It skimmed, no: it
flowed like water, over the shoulder of the statue,
smoothly caressing the curve of the neck, the coastal
line of her jaw, her cheek, the planes of her temples.
There, in the moonlit dark, was his mother.

"The king had asked him to carve a statue of the
most beautiful woman ever and the marble had brought
forth his mother.

"The next day he was in his studio, holding the

smallest of his chisels, and pretended not to hear the king when he entered. Satisfaction and envy fought each other in the king's face as he looked at the marble foot that appeared from under the great piece of cloth that covered most of the statue. 'Almost finished, master sculptor?' His voice rang through the high room. The artist turned around and wiped the dust from his brows. 'It's hard to tell, my lord. It's not finding the shape that's the hardest, but bringing it forth.' A deep frown wrinkled the king's brow. He walked toward the statue and reached out to remove the cloth, but the sculptor blocked his way. 'Forgive me, but it isn't finished yet.' The ruler of the island turned away with a hurt look on his face. 'But how long will it take, master?' he asked. The old sculptor thought for a while and finally said: 'It could be days. It could be months.' The king gasped for air, like a fish out of water. 'But with a chisel like that!' he roared. The artist looked at it and nodded. Then he said: 'My lord, how do you rule your country? With an army, or with a few well-placed servants?' The king stared at him for a while, then left the dusty studio, muttering as he went."

I drink my tea. This is the sign. Eleven staring faces suddenly remember their Cokes and juice. Behind the raised glasses the smoky arabesque of Nur's Marlboro Light ascends.

"Days, weeks went by, and every time the king visited the sculptor's studio, the old man was hacking away with a chisel no bigger than a teaspoon. And every time, the king, snorting with rage, returned to the great hall, where he would yell at his master onion peeler or the royal sock mender. The king's mood gradually worsened. He'd lost his appetite and nights he lay awake, even though the beautiful girls sat around his bed and sang and softly strummed the strings of their lutes and lyres. And when he finally, after hours of tossing and turning, closed his eyes, he invariably saw the pale marble figure from the studio floating through the dark corridors of the palace, till it was quite close, which was when he saw that it was faceless.

"It was autumn and the painted trees on the pillars shed their leaves; the sky on the ceiling of the great hall turned gray and moved like a sea of lead.

"One day the old sculptor asked his son to join him. It was a windy day and they sat on the wide windowsill, looking out over the bay that lapped at the foot of the palace walls and stretched out into the sea.

" 'Listen, boy,' the father said. 'The king will throw in one of his dungeons, or worse, once the statue is finished. I have designed a scheme to save us, however, but it will fail unless you do exactly as told.' The boy nodded and listened to his father, who began to tell his plan.

"A few days later the artist sent word to the king that he was ready to show his work. The king, three of his most loyal servants trailing behind him, hurried through the palace corridors, his robes streaming. His dignity didn't allow him to run, but that was what he really wanted to do. The windows of the studio were hung with heavy curtains. A few chandeliers shed their light on a figure that was almost completely hidden by a curtain hanging from a cord between two walls. The king and his servants stopped abruptly when they saw all this. The sculptor raised his hand and cried: 'Right there, Your Majesty. Not any farther!' The king's face clouded over. 'My statue, master sculptor,' he said. 'Show me my statue.' The artist nodded and said: 'Our statue, my lord, and you will see it. But alone. Send your servants away, so that you will truly be the first one in the world to see the most beautiful woman.' The king stared long and hard at the sculptor, then sent his companions away. He crossed his arms in front of his chest and curtly nodded. The sculptor accompanied him to an armchair and the king reluctantly sat down. 'No more dallying, master. Show me the statue.' The old man nodded, stepped back, and bowed his head.

"The curtain opened slowly and the white contours

of the marble took shape in the shimmering light of the candles. The king sighed. 'You've outdone yourself, old man,' he said. He nodded for some time. 'It's almost as if it is alive.' He closed his eyes, stretched out his left hand in the direction of the statue, and murmured something in a strange tongue. The curtains at the windows started to move, as if a sudden gust of wind had entered the room, and the fabric that hung on both sides of the statue tugged at the cord. The king pressed the fingers of his right hand against his temples and kept uttering unrecognizable words. The statue shivered, and a soft moan seemed to escape from the marble.

"The studio was in a turmoil now: chisels moved across the floor, pieces of cloth billowed, flames roared above their candles. The king braced himself in his chair and shouted a word.

"Suddenly there was stillness in the air. The statue looked about and bowed its head. 'Where is my master?' it said, after a while. 'Here!' the king cried. 'I am your master.' The statue shook its head. 'I am your master!' the king roared.

"The sculptor stepped out of the shadows. His son stood next to him, holding a rope that seemed to disappear in shadows overhead. The statue turned to the old man and held out its arms. 'What is this?' the king cried. 'What have you done to my statue, you impostor?' The sculptor smiled. 'I have let you do something to my statue, lord. Please, stay seated, and don't call for your servants. My son could let go of this rope and something might drop.' The king looked up and saw a sharply pointed sword over his head. He hissed angrily. The sculptor and his son went to the statue, stood in front of it, and were grabbed by two marble arms. Then they were lifted up. The king, who involuntarily looked up, saw the sword move. The statue stepped forward and only now the king saw what the curtains had covered: on the back of the marble figure were two wings, so tall that they brushed the floor. 'Take us home,' said the sculptor. The statue nodded gravely. It lifted the old man and his son little higher, the sword dropped a few feet, and the statue proceeded toward one of the windows. The king rushed out of his chair. He heard a noise, like a gust of wind, and suddenly couldn't move anymore. The curtains in front of the windows parted and the image, carrying her creator and his son, stepped out. When the king looked back, he saw that the sword had fallen and nailed his robes to the chair. He yelled for his guard, tore himself loose, and ran to the window. An angel soared high above the bay, clutching two men against her breast."

After the silence come the questions. "What was the son called? Where did they go? What did they do with the statue?" I just shake my head and raise my hand like a thoughtful stationmaster. "Fairy tales aren't meant to answer questions. Time to go, anyway. Look what we've done. Or, rather, what we didn't do. Next week, we'll finish building these kites and if the weather's good, we'll fly them. We'll go to the seashore and if the winds are favorable we will let them go and think they're angels. Time to clean up now. All of you." (A short glance at Abdel, who still sits with the sphere in his hand and, eyes soft with yearning, looks at the minuscule airplane inside, fighting its way through a blizzard.)

Five o'clock, and the children leave. Nur sees them to the door and waves, she says something in a strange language, and they all laugh, they run-tumble-tug around the corner and dissolve into the crowd in the street. I clean up the shop, flip the sign behind the glass in the door, and sweep clean the workbench. Nur leans against the chest that holds the blueprints and smokes.

"Shall we eat?"

"Later," she says. She stubs out her cigarette and unbuttons her coat. The red of her blouse blushes like a peony. I carry an armful of bits and pieces of cut-up kite fabric and am a man in love. "Come," I say. "Let's go and have a drink on the veranda. The weather's fine." And I think: Even after two years of being together I'm still to shy to say, let me lay you down, here, on the table, and kiss your breasts.

I am a reluctant man when it comes to women. If it had been up to me, it would have taken at least ten years before we ever started something.

She was researching small businesses in the city and came around to ask questions. I'd burst out laughing when she explained the purpose of her visit, but I invited her in and made tea. We'd sat in the workshop, at a table that was littered with scissors, knives, countless pieces of string and snippets of nylon. It soon was clear that I'd hardly be "relevant research material." But she stayed nevertheless, and drank tea for two hours, and my eyes rested longer and longer on her eyes in the course of those two hours, they rested on the curve of her cheekbone, the pencil-drawn contour of her mouth, her heavy black hair.

"How does someone become a kite builder?" she had asked.

"I was a doll doctor to start with," I said.

"Why does a doll doctor take up kite building?"

"I hated dolls."

She'd sighed and blown her hair out of her face. She had opened her shiny black briefcase, taken out her cigarettes, and checked her mobile.

"How does someone get to be a pollster?" I asked.

"I'm not a pollster. I studied law. I'm doing a . . ."

"Okay, okay."

We didn't speak for a while. Then I said: "If we go for dinner, we could explain why we are what we do."

She had looked at me with a deep frown in the elegant curves above her eyes and my stomach felt dizzy.

And we went out and had dinner in one of those hip new restaurants she knew, where the entrée was a small layered structure and the main course had to be eaten clockwise, or the other way around, and one week later she entered the shop at five o'clock, carrying a bag filled to the brim with groceries, and said she was going to cook for me. That night, sprawled on the couch, watching the video she'd brought and drinking a New Zealand Riesling, she said: "I've thought it over and I will do it."

"What?" I said. "What will you do?"

She wrapped her right leg around me, lowered herself on my lap, and said: "I am going to love you."

That was two years ago.

"How come," I'd asked her, "a young thirty-year-old woman fancies a forty-year-old Jewish doll doctor?"

"Turkish young woman," she said.

"Turkish young woman. Jewish doll doctor."

"Kite builder."

"Why!"

"Because you're a strange man."

I could only nod.

"Because you let me lead my own life, not because you're afraid to lose me, but because you believe in it."

"I'm a wonderful man."

"You're a jerk, but you're my jerk."

"Never heard a better reason."

Nur, I gathered, could show me the way. And she did.

And now, with our bottle of white wine, on the veranda, staring at the houses on the other side of the little park and the boys and girls playing football, now she says: "You never told me where you got that sphere that Abdel is always playing with."

"You never asked me."

"Do you think you'll tell me?"

"My father and I played a game, whenever we sat here. We would look at the windows, over there, and we'd try to guess what they'd be doing, those people in their little lamplit boxes on the other side of the park. But you weren't allowed to just say it. You had to act."

She smiles, tilts her head back slightly, and closes her eyes. I dip a finger in the wine and touch her lips with it. She briefly opens them and licks.

"My father," I tell her, "had quit his job. It was summer and he and the doll doctor, who had his shop downstairs, sat on the balcony, drinking beer. The doll doctor sold model airplanes too, probably because deep down he hated dolls."

A couple of houses away the loud wailing of Chinese karaoke starts in the restaurant where, earlier today, wedding guests from all over Europe arrived. The smell of lamb cutlets and thyme escapes from the kitchen of the illegal joint next door.

"He used to get boys in his shop who'd ask if they could have a ready-made model. That's what they were talking about, the doll doctor and my father, when I had an idea. Actually, it was a plan. It was the plan that would save us."